Thief Taker

by the same author

Dirty Weekend

Thief Taker

Alan Scholefield

St. Martin's Press
New York

Library of Congress Cataloging-in-Publication Data

Scholefield, Alan.
    Thief taker / Alan Scholefield.
        p.   cm.
    ISBN 0-312-08320-3
    I. Title.
    PR9369.3.S43T47   1992
    823—dc20   92-19681
                                                                      CIP

First published in Great Britain by Macmillan London Limited.

First U.S. Edition: September 1992
10 9 8 7 6 5 4 3 2 1

ACKNOWLEDGEMENTS

My thanks for their help go to:
Dr Robin Ilbert
and to
Detective Inspector Hugh Toomer
of the Metropolitan Police (retired).

Any mistakes are my own.

Chapter 1

At 11.42 a.m. a millionaire called Robson Healey made a phone call from his Chelsea home.

'Hello, this is—'

'No names, please,' a man's voice said.

'OK. Sorry. I forgot.'

'Do you have a client number?'

'Thirty-seven.'

'I'll just bring that up. Oh, yes. Fine. What may I do for you?'

'What d'you think? I'm not phoning just for a bloody chat.'

'Any particular one?'

'The one I had last time.'

'One moment. Yes. Lucy. She's free. What time, sir?'

'Six-ish.'

'Do you wish her to bring anything special?'

'Like?'

'Well, sir, in the past she has brought—'

'No, nothing special, not this time. But I'll want her for the whole night.'

'Very well, sir. Six o'clock unless you hear from me. Thank you for your call and have a nice day.'

It *was* a nice day.

London on a sunny Sunday in spring.

The daffodils were out in Hyde Park. So were the old folk, walking arm in arm.

The young were out too; kids sailing their boats on the

Round Pond; even younger kids, with their dads, feeding the ducks in St James's Park.

The riders were out in Rotten Row. Soccer was giving way to cricket.

Joggers were out and so were young women looking for a suntan.

Ice-cream sellers were out.

Lovers were out, and in the parks you had to step over them. Tourists were out and in the Underground stations you had to push past them while they sorted out their currency.

In Covent Garden the buskers were out; jugglers, and fire-eaters, and music students playing Bach.

In Bond Street and Regent Street the window-shoppers were out.

And in Whitehall cyclists were out for a race which would soon paralyse London's traffic.

Everyone was out.

Even the killers.

It was a nice day for murder.

Chapter 2

'It's a naïve, domestic burgundy without any breeding,' Zoe Bertram said, pulling out the cork of a bottle of red wine. 'But I think you'll be surprised by its presumption.'

'Amused,' Leo Silver said.

'What?'

'Amused by its presumption.'

It was early evening on that same spring Sunday and they were in their maisonette in Pimlico. Zoe had recently returned from visiting her father in Surrey and had brought back a bottle of wine.

'Everybody gets that quotation wrong,' Leo said.

'Except you!'

'Except me.'

'You're always correcting me these days. *I* told you about Thurber. He was *mine*. Now *you've* taken him over. You're always taking over my things.'

'It's still "amused".'

'Where's the book? We'll look it up.'

'I lent it to Macrae.'

'It's *my* book, Leo. Anyway, what would Macrae want with it?'

'Don't kid yourself. Macrae's got shelves of books at his house, *and* he's read them all. Once asked me if I'd read any Dickens. He loves Dickens.'

'And I suppose he cries at the death of Little Nell.' She gave him a glass of wine.

The thought of Macrae crying at *anything* did not come easily to Leo. 'No, I don't think so.'

Detective Sergeant Leopold Silver was in his late twenties and was dressed sharply in black: black brogues, black trousers, black polo-neck and there was a black leather jacket hanging in the hall.

The apartment was a mixture of yellows and greens and browns, splashy colours that even in winter gave it a summery look.

Zoe had chosen the colours when she and Silver had begun living together. They suited her. She was small and dark with a brownish skin, large wide-spaced brown eyes, high cheekbones and a thin, restless body. She looked, Silver always thought, like a South American with just a touch of Indian.

Exotic.

She came and sat beside him on the apricot-coloured sofa and rubbed his cheek with the back of her hand. 'How's the family?'

Leo's family meant The Silvers. That's how Zoe thought of them: in capital letters. Whenever he could, Leo had Sunday lunch with his father and mother and sister and brother-in-law and nephew. Zoe took the opportunity to visit her own father. She didn't have to go quite so regularly but was glad in a way to escape Leo's argumentative, opinionated and bickering relations.

Leo had had to make excuses for her today, just as he made them most Sundays as they sat down to lunch in the large untidy apartment on the wrong side of the Finchley Road in north-west London.

'Zoe never comes on a Sunday,' his father Manfred had said, beginning to carve the roast beef. 'We never see her.'

'She goes to see her own father on Sundays,' Leo said.

'Every Sunday?' his sister Ruth asked. She was a large, bespectacled woman some years older than Leo, who wore wooden beads and sandals and a purple dress in between.

'We like to see ours whenever we can, don't we?'

'Thank you,' (Zank yew) his mother Lottie said. 'You're a good boy.'

10

The senior Silvers (née Silberbauers) were Austrian immigrants who retained their heavy accents.

Now Leo said to Zoe, 'It would be nice if you'd come for lunch one Sunday. I think they think you don't want to come.'

'Why?'

'God knows. You know Dad.'

'I know he washes his hands all the time.'

Leo laughed. 'There's nothing Freudian in that. It's just he's used to it. Piano teachers like to have clean hands.'

'Leo . . . do they ever talk about me? You know . . . '

'Well, they ask after you. That's only natural. Why?'

'I just wondered.'

He was lying. The subject of Sunday visiting had hardly come up when Ruth had said to Leo. 'Are you going to marry Zoe?'

Like a volley at the net he had replied, 'Are you going to divorce Sidney?'

His brother-in-law made a choking sound.

'Are you mad?' Ruth had said. 'What sort of question is that?'

'A personal question. The sort you just asked me.'

It wasn't the sort of exchange he could explain to Zoe.

'How was *your* father?' Leo asked.

'He's OK. He's thinking of taking up golf. Last year it was wine-making. Next year, God knows.'

'He should take up fishing. You can do that by yourself.'

'What does the family think?'

'About what?'

'About *you* going fishing? I bet no one on either side has ever gone fishing before. It's not something that Jews seem to do.'

'Sidney thinks I'm going to catch turbot.'

She laughed then said, 'What are you really going to catch?'

'I'm going to *try* to catch a salmon.'

'I thought they always came in packets.'

11

'Only when they're smoked.'

'Right. And you've got to catch them first.'

'Right.'

'God Leo, you're so *clever!*'

He ignored the sarcasm and went to fetch a short spinning rod on which there was a four-inch wooden minnow containing three barbed hooks attached to the end of the nylon line.

'It's Macrae's,' he said. 'He lent it to me. See the reel? It's called a fixed spool, whatever that means.'

'And you throw that piece of wood into the water and then the salmon eats it and you reel it in. Right?'

'The word is cast. Not throw. I cast in the minnow . . . See? It's painted to look like a little fish . . . '

His mind suddenly went back a few evenings to the lawns on the Thames Embankment outside Cannon Row police station. Macrae had taken him out in a light drizzle to teach him how to cast.

'No, no, laddie, not like that!' He'd shouted as Silver managed to cast the minnow round the neck of General Gordon, the hero of Khartoum, whose statue stared south across the river.

'Watch what you're doing! I told you, the fish are lying with their heads to the current. You cast the minnow upstream and then let it come down and as it swings past you – that's when he'll take it. That's if he's a bloody fool.'

Zoe said, 'I can't wait. You realise it'll be the first time we've been away properly. How shall we register? Mr and Mrs Smith? I've always wanted to.'

'Why not?'

'Or Mr and Mrs Silver?'

He wondered if this was as innocent as it sounded. She hadn't touched on the question of marriage for some time. And he hadn't brought it up. It was one of the reasons he was glad she visited her father when he went to see his family. It would be just like Ruth or his parents to blunder in with some question like, 'When are you two getting married?' He wasn't

12

sure that either Manfred or Lottie had quite got used to the openness with which people lived together these days.

And what would he have said? That he wasn't ready for marriage yet? That he wanted to move up in the police hierarchy before contemplating the finality of connubial bliss and children? That wouldn't have been very bright even if it was true.

'You want to see my country clothes for walking along river-banks, Leo?'

'Haven't you got any new underwear?'

'I have, actually.'

'I'd rather see that.'

She came back with a Next bag and pulled out several pieces of lingerie.

'Jesus, what's that?' Silver said, as she held up something edged with black lace.

'It's called a Teddy. You want to see me in it?'

She pulled off her shirt. Her smallish breasts, as Silver never tired of remarking, were fruity. They reminded him of all kinds of lovely, fruity things.

She was about to remove her pants when he turned to the window and said to the house across the street. 'Oh, hi. You want to see the show?'

'There's no one there,' Zoe said. 'The windows are dark. But just because you're such a prude . . . ' She drew the curtains.

Silver watched her with more than academic interest. She had no false modesty and this, more than anything, turned him on.

'Come over here,' he said.

At that moment the phone rang. He picked it up. 'Yes? Yes. OK. Five minutes.'

Zoe paused halfway across the yellow carpet. Her breasts were firm and hard, the nipples pointing at him, not so much like fruit, but crossly, like Luger pistols. 'It *always* happens!'

He held her and kissed her. 'Don't go away,' he said. 'Raincheck.'

He swallowed another glass of wine and grabbed a piece of bread and cheese. He didn't know when he'd be eating next.

She put on her shirt and was buttoning it slowly. Tears were trickling down her cheeks. 'Even on a Sunday night,' she said.

'I know. But people get murdered on Sundays too.'

He held her tight. 'Only a few more days. Can you hang on? Then no one'll find us.'

Her face was crushed against his black leather jacket and she did not reply.

There was a toot from the street below. 'That'll be Eddie,' he said. 'I've got to go.'

He let himself out of the apartment and heard her locking and relocking the three deadlocks that turned the place into a fortress. Then he was in the street. Except for Eddie Twyford in the unmarked police car, it was deserted. Eddie grunted hello and said they were going to pick up Macrae. They made for Battersea Bridge.

14

Chapter 3

It was the early-evening booze-up at the Blind Pig in Battersea and the bars were crowded.

Detective Superintendent George Macrae was slightly drunk. Not staggering. Or blurred. But floating just a few inches off the ground. His tongue and mouth had reached that state when every draw of his cigar tasted better than the last; and when the woman at his side was affecting him – as she had affected him before – like a dirty postcard.

Her name was Mandy Parrish. She was in her thirties, big-bodied, fleshy in an overripe way, with thick black hair and a handsome face.

She wore tight-fitting jeans which clung to her buttocks and thighs like paint, and a shocking pink blouse that stretched tight against her heavy, loose breasts.

Macrae knew those breasts intimately, he knew the colour of the areolae and the delicate shading of the nipples. He knew just how they felt in the hand. Mandy Parrish had once been Woman Police Constable Mandy Macrae, his second wife.

Macrae was a big man, dressed conventionally in grey slacks, shirt and tie, and a tweed sports jacket. He stood out against the other drinkers who were wearing – in what passed in the Blind Pig for leisure gear – dirty trainers, denims and rolled gold chains.

She held a cheque in her fingers, looked at it and folded it away.

'Thanks,' she said. 'I wish it was always this early.'

'If I hadn't given it to you now I'd have spent it.'

She lit a cigarette. 'You know, George, it'll have to go up a bit. I can't manage on this. I mean the kids are growing up, they need things.'

'I know.'

It had been 'his' day yesterday. He had taken Bobbie and Margaret to the zoo and become increasingly aware that he wasn't much of a father any more. More of an uncle or a cousin. Bobbie was nine and Margaret seven, and they seemed to need each other more than they needed him. He had spent the day trailing along behind them, watching animals being fed. Then he had fed his children. Over the meal they talked about little except television programmes they had seen. He hardly watched TV so they had no real common ground. By the time they had finished their ice-creams they had become restless and he had taken them home.

'Have another,' he said to Mandy.

'I should be getting back.'

'What time do you eat?'

'About seven.'

'It's past that now. What about the kids?'

'Oh, Joe'll get them something.'

'How are you and Joe getting on?'

'What business is it of yours?'

'None at all. Sorry.'

'Oh hell, no need. He's OK. Kind. A decent sort of bloke. And he thinks the world of me. *And* tells me so. *And* comes home at night – which you didn't.'

'You knew what the Force was like. You should've, anyway.'

'Yeah, but he needs me. You never needed anyone. That was your trouble, George. You married the Force and became the great thief taker before you married either Linda or me. Anyway, Joe's a good husband and he's good with the kids. You don't have to worry about that. And he's doing all right in a quiet sort of way. He's never going to be the Mr Big of the taxi-cab business but we'll be all right. It's just . . . '

16

'What?'

'Oh, you know . . . With you it wasn't all sweetness and light. You're a bastard when you want to be. But . . . when we had it going the walls could have fallen in and we wouldn't have noticed. But Joe . . . Well, he's not exactly Tarzan.'

'No.'

'I suppose saying that's bloody disloyal. But it's true. Anyway, there's this other bloke. Two doors down. Works nights so he's about during the day.'

'Single lad?'

'No, married. But his wife works days.'

'You like him?'

'I dunno really. We don't talk much.'

'Just the old one-two.'

'That's right, George, just the old one-two.' She looked at him sideways under her lids. 'Not jealous, are you?'

He had an overriding urge to put out his hand and fondle her breasts.

'What about that drink?'

'Why not?'

'Two more,' Macrae said, turning his heavy head towards the barman.

Harassed, and already taking an order, the barman snapped, 'Can't you see I'm— Oh, sorry, Mr Macrae.' He dropped the other customer and came quickly down the bar. 'Gin and tonics, was it?'

'Large ones.'

'You'll have me pissed,' Mandy said.

'You remember that office party? The one—'

'The one when we were drinking Manhattans? And we did it in a broom cupboard?'

'It wasn't a broom cupboard.'

'Well, it smelled of wet mops and we couldn't lie down.'

'And that time in Streatham. On the observation.'

'I remember. In the car. God . . . I dunno how the kids manage. No cars for me any more.'

17

He smiled at her. 'You shouldn't have to. You're built for comfort not for speed.'

The present reasserted itself. 'But I'm serious, George. The kids *are* growing up. And the money isn't enough.'

'What about something to eat?' he said, changing the subject.

'Here?' Her mouth turned down.

'There's an Indian take-away down the street. We could go to my place. It's not far.'

'I know where it is, George. I lived there too, remember?'

They bought a couple of bottles of Liebfraumilch then went to the take-away and George bought two vindaloos, stuffed parathas, rice, onion bagees, mixed vegetables and two large helpings of lime pickle and mango chutney. The drinks had made them hungry and the smell of the bubbling curries was almost too much to bear.

His terraced house was in a street that looked as though it had been the centre of a recent tank battle. Rubble and rusting cars and graffiti of the Belfast-school of wall artists gave the place a flavour of Northern Ireland.

Mandy stopped at the door before following him in. 'I thought Battersea was coming up in the world,' she said.

The house looked what it was, the lair of a single man who did not notice his surroundings. But both were too drunk to care.

He opened the cardboard containers and poured the contents on to plates. She was half leaning on the kitchen table. His arm brushed against her breasts as he moved and that was the trigger. He found himself shaking. He caught her arms and she came up to him as though on springs. They kissed and in a second were pulling at each other's clothing. His hand slipped under her blouse and covered one of her breasts. He felt her fingers on his trousers. As they wrestled they fell against the table which moved under their weight.

'Not here!' she said, sliding her mouth away from his. 'Not on the floor!'

They climbed the stairs, shedding pieces of clothing as they went. His bed was still unmade but neither noticed that. He went down on top of her like a bull.

It was all over for both of them in less than a couple of minutes and they lay together, hearts racing, breath coming in gusts, finally slowing down to a kind of free-floating numbness.

'Jesus, George!'

'Aye . . . That's what we've been missing.'

After a few minutes she got up and brought the curries into the bedroom. He opened a bottle of wine. Both of them sat naked on the bed, eating and drinking.

When they'd finished she said. 'I'd better go.'

'What'll you say to Joe?'

'He won't ask.' She made up her face. 'Getting back to the kids. I'll need at least another twenty a week.'

He did not reply and she kissed him on the mouth. 'Thanks for everything.'

He lay in bed after she left, smoking and looking at the ceiling. Money. It all came down to money. Three thousand quid he'd had to find for Susan, his daughter by his first marriage, to go gallivanting around South-East Asia with her boyfriend.

He remembered the night his first wife had asked him for it. She'd looked so good then, so different from the little Linda Brown he had married. That's who he should have been having supper with this evening and not getting pissed at a boozer first. And not take-aways, but a proper meal in a proper restaurant and then . . . perhaps back to her place, not this pit.

He'd hoped that meeting was the beginning of something, but he'd got mixed up with a bunch of crazy Triads* and by the time the case was over . . . well, somehow, he hadn't had the courage to ring her.

* *Dirty Weekend* by Alan (A. T.) Scholefield (St. Martin's Press, 1991)

19

Soon he was telling himself she'd only met him to talk about the money for Susan. That way he could dislike her.

Money. Everybody wanted his money.

He remembered the bank manager's face when he'd asked for a loan. He'd paused, put on his glasses, looked at the papers on the desk and said, 'Your house has a second mortgage on it, Mr Macrae. I'm afraid that under our regulations we are not able to make you a loan. Indeed your overdraft . . . ' He flicked at the figures like a schoolmaster marking shoddy homework.

And so he had found the money elsewhere. He didn't like to think about where. And now Mandy wanted more for the kids . . .

Anyway, to hell with it. Don't think about it. Think about Linda instead. Life wasn't just sex, he told himself. It was companionship. Friendship.

That's what he'd had with Linda.

The sex had been with Mandy.

Chapter 4

'Ron! Where are you, Ron?'

You old cow, he said under his breath. Bloody old cow.

He had the gun on his bed. It lay in several parts; the barrel, the grip, the magazine, the bullets.

He was having a little exhibition, just for himself. Spread out on the pink candlewick bedspread was the SS cap badge, the Iron Cross (Third Class), the pair of Zeiss binoculars said to have belonged to one of Rommel's staff officers (a lens was missing which was why he had got them cheap), the red silk flag with the black swastika in the middle, the death star he'd found at the martial arts shop in the Charing Cross Road, the flick-knife he'd bought on a day trip to France.

His 'Collection'.

He'd thought of it many times. Dozens. Hundreds. Lying on his bed listening to old Crowhurst snoring and muttering in his sleep, he'd thought of each piece detail by detail and had promised himself that the first thing he'd do when he got out was have one of his old exhibitions.

And that's what he'd done.

'Isn't it time for my pill?' His mother's voice came through from her bedroom next door. 'You know what the doctor said.'

I know the doctor said you'd never bloody walk again, that's what I know, Ron said to her, or would have said to her, or wished he was able to say to her. Instead he said it to himself.

'Ron!'

'I'm not Ron!' he shouted. 'I've told you a thousand times! Ronnie. Ronald. Mr Purvis. Not Ron!'

'Mr Purvis? You must be mad. You're my own son. I'm not going to call you Mr Purvis!'

'Well, don't call me Ron then!'

Otherwise I'll smother you, you old cow.

His 'Collection' had once been ten times its present size. The coppers had got most of it, but not the cream. He'd buried these in next-door's garden months before he'd been arrested, just a hole and a concrete slab to cover them. 'Course the coppers never thought of looking next door. Why should they?

Old Mrs Blunt had lived there ever since his family had moved to London when he was a kid. Half blind, she was, and deaf as a post. She'd seen him there once, getting out the plastic box, and he'd said he was looking for his ball.

'Don't you go breaking my windows,' she'd said.

He'd been twenty-something but she still thought of him as a little kid. Which was good. It meant he could climb into her small back garden almost any time, and if she did see him – *if* – he'd just go on about losing his ball.

If the pieces on the bed were the cream of the collection, then the pistol was the 'cream de la cream' as Crowhurst was always saying with a leer – the bloody old bender. And ignorant too.

Browning automatic pistol. Made in Belgium. Gun-metal black with cross-hatching on the grip. A 'revolver', his mother had called it when she saw it the one and only time. Jesus Christ, a *revolver*. Who did she think he was, Billy the Kid? He'd tried to explain the difference between a pistol and a revolver but she'd been just about bloody hysterical.

'I don't care *what* it is! I just want you to get rid of it!'

Made him promise to take it that *instant* to the police station.

'And tell them where you picked it up!'

Naturally he hadn't gone anywhere near the police station. He'd set off down the road and then come home the back way through old Mrs Blunt's yard – and that's when the idea came.

That night he'd dug a hole and put the gun and his other things in a plastic box and hidden it there.

Buried treasure. Brilliant.

'Ronald!'

She's learning.

But he wasn't ready yet. He had the gun oil. Ballistol. They said it was so pure you could gargle with it, rub it on cuts. They said it was a magic cure-all. He worked the breech. Lovely smooth action. Pulled the trigger. Click . . . click . . . firm . . . solid . . . He put some oil on the rag and began to rub the barrel up and down . . . up and down . . . The smell was lovely. Up and down . . . slow . . . then quicker . . .

'Ronnie!'

'What?'

'I told you. My pill. Anyway I need to go.'

'You went half an hour ago.'

'I can't help it.' Pause. 'You don't think I *want* to be like this, do you?' Pause. '*Do you?*' It was a shriek.

'Oh Christ, all right.'

He stopped by the long mirror near the door and looked at himself. Medium height, thin, sharp-featured. Ratty, they'd called him at school. His fingers strayed to the livid scar on his left cheekbone. Depressed fracture of the maxilla, the doctor had said. Broken nose, he'd said. Numbness, he'd said. And he was right. He still couldn't feel his upper lip, still couldn't breathe properly. He'd grown his hair long to try and cover the scar. 'Veronica', Crowhurst had called him. Veronica bloody Lake.

At first he'd been angry, then he found that many of the Rule 43 prisoners had female names. Crowhurst himself was called 'Jill'. Imagine that. And him an elderly geezer and ex-army. Still, he hadn't minded calling him 'Jill' if that's what turned him on. He didn't even mind being called 'Veronica' himself as long as they didn't try to interfere with him. But they had, of course. Or tried to. Rule 43 prisoners always did.

Before he was put in with Crowhurst he'd shared with a

bloke called Flugl . . . Flugel – something like that – big sod who was in for messing about with a kid. And so anyway this bloke tried to mess about with him and Ronnie had said OK, mate, you do that again and I'm going to think of something. And Flugel had laughed at him and done it again and when he was asleep Ronnie had held a pillow over his face until Flugel woke up choking. 'Course he'd bashed Ronnie, but he'd persevered. He'd done it three nights in a row and Flugel got to a point where he wouldn't go to sleep. After that he left Ronnie alone.

He took his mum to the bathroom and helped her back into bed.

'And now my pill,' she said.

He gave her a white pill and some water. She had more pills than he could count. Red ones and blue ones; white ones and brown ones. Pills to alleviate pain. Pills to combat high blood pressure. Pills to bring down the rheumatic swellings in her joints. Pills for this and pills for that and pills to stop her stomach rotting from all the other pills.

'You take more pills than—'

'You should be thankful for the pills. If it wasn't for the pills you'd still be inside. God, when I think what you could have been! What I worked and scraped for!'

He didn't want to get into the what-I-sacrificed-for-you bit.

'Why should I be grateful?'

'If it wasn't for my illness they'd never have given you early parole. Never. Nearest relative. That's you.' She turned away.

What a difference, he thought. She'd been a big, masculine woman, with powerful, knotted legs. Powerful personality too. Much too powerful for his dad. Now look at her. Long, grey, untidy hair, sagging flesh, loose dentures.

'Nothing to do with you needing looking after.'

'Plump them up a bit.'

He plumped up her pillows.

'What then?' she snapped sullenly.

'The therapy at Granton.'

24

'The madhouse? Don't make me laugh!'

'That's just the sort of thing you *would* say. It's not a madhouse. It's a psychological unit for prisoners who *want* to improve.'

'You believe that you'll believe anything.' She settled back. 'Anyway, you're home. And now you've got to do your duty.'

'What duty's that?'

'Looking after me. That's what. Just like I looked after your grandmother.'

'That wasn't long.'

'Eighteen months it was before she died.'

'Father said it was twelve.'

'How would he have known?'

Ronnie could hear the contempt in her voice and he didn't like it. Didn't do to speak ill of the dead.

'Bring the TV nearer,' she said.

She was settling down for the evening. Good, he thought.

'Any more pills?'

'The blue ones. But not till nine.'

'I may be out at nine.'

'Out! And leave me! What for?'

He might have told her to post a letter. But she'd want to know every last bloody detail about it and it wasn't her business.

'There doesn't have to be a reason. Out. Just so I'm not in all the bloody time.'

'And stop your swearing. When I think how I slaved to send you to a private school!'

'That place! You could've saved your money.'

'There was nothing wrong with it.'

'There was everything wrong with it. Pretended to have a history and traditions. The bloody place was only founded after the war.'

'It was a good school and you should have got on. Instead . . . and just listen to you. Bloody this and bloody that. You didn't pick that up at school. You got that from your prisoner pals.'

25

'Wormwood Scrubs. University of Life. BA Degree in Buggery. Like to see the tie?'

'Don't be cheeky! I'm your mother!'

It was time to stop. They both knew it because they had come to this point so many times before. They stared at each other like a mongoose and a snake. If Ronnie was the mongoose, his mother was like a large constrictor. The mongoose had sharp teeth but the constrictor's coils had been round him since birth.

'I think I'll have my medicine now,' she said, suddenly arch.

'Your sundowner?'

She smiled at him. 'Yes, darling, my sundowner.'

He went to get the sherry. He liked her to call him darling. It sounded sophisticated; the way people spoke to each other in the movies. In his whole life, which was twenty-nine years, no one but his mother had ever called him darling.

He came back with the sherry. The bottle was half full.

'That's all there is,' he said.

A look of alarm crossed her face. 'What about the other one. I thought there were two?'

'You drank the other one last night. *And* half of this one.'

She smiled like a little girl. 'That was naughty, wasn't it?'

She wasn't supposed to drink with all the pills she was taking, but you couldn't blame her, he thought. The trouble was she got so bloody pissed he had to be around when it was pill time. Otherwise God knew what she'd take. Once before she made herself so ill taking handfuls of the things that the doctor had asked him to dole them out.

'Ronnie?'

'Yeah?'

'When you go out, get me another.' She pointed to the bottle.

'OK.'

She switched on the TV, turned away and settled against her pillows, the glass and bottle to hand. He opened his mouth to say something but she was no longer aware he was in the room.

Chapter 5

The house was in one of the elegant little squares off the King's Road in Chelsea; three storeys and a basement in a terrace of identical houses, all painted white, all with doors either shiny black or yellow or deep purple, all with heavy brass door furniture, all with bars on the windows.

Expensive cages.

This particular house, number thirty-three on the west side, had security bars on every window and an alarm box on the wall. This was how Zoe would like to live, Silver had thought when he and Macrae had arrived earlier in the evening.

It was now almost midnight.

There was a great deal to protect: the ground-floor hall was hung with paintings: Braque, Klimt, and Mondrian – the value of which Silver could not even begin to assess. In the living room he saw two Picassos and a Dufy and there was a Léger and a 'Douanier' Rousseau in the first-floor study. The walls of the bathroom and lavatory were covered by erotic art: Beardsley and Egon Schiele, Indian miniatures and Japanese scroll drawings. The main bedroom was devoid of all paintings but it did have a complete mirror wall.

It also had the body.

The corpse lay on the white carpet at the foot of the bed. At first Silver had thought that the carpet was patterned. Then he saw that the patterns were splashes and trickles of blood. A large area was speckled with tiny red droplets and so was a section of the mirror-wall, as though someone had given it a burst from an aerosol containing red paint.

The body, in death as in life, had a name: Robson Healey, and Macrae had recognised it instantly.

Shipping.

The police procedure was in full swing: the doctor had been, the police photographer had been, Forensic was combing the place and the 'blue serge' – or 'woodentops' as Macrae disparagingly called the uniformed branch – who had arrived first, were still saturating the house. An incident room was in the process of being set up at Cannon Row police station, and everything was going just beautifully – except for Robson Healey and the fact that no one knew who had killed him, for killed he had certainly been.

'A blow to the head with a blunt instrument,' Silver had said, unconsciously cathartic.

The duty doctor, an elderly man called Dr Willey, who had been wrenched away from the bridge table and who was in no mood for levity, had snarled, 'For goodness sake, man, have you no feelings!'

Silver had been taken aback. This was not the first murder victim he had seen. He had been badly affected by the early ones. Now, he realised, he was making jokes about them.

Before the body was zipped into a body-bag, Silver studied it carefully. Healey had a young-old face, deeply suntanned. You didn't usually get tanned in an English spring and it spoke of a yacht in the Med or a sunlamp. His white hair was heavy and thick, exceptionally so for a man in late middle-age. Now it was disfigured by blood and bits of flesh and bone, and what might have been brains. When he died he was wearing clothes more suitable for St Tropez than London on a damp night: blue espadrilles, light blue cotton trousers, a blue denim shirt and the mandatory gold chain around his neck. He looked more like a cliché Hollywood producer than a British shipping magnate.

'Fractured,' Dr Willey said, pointing to the skull. 'Probably a hair-line crack. Which explains the spray. Been hit half a dozen times at least. But even that didn't kill him immediately. That's why there's all the blood.'

'How long could he have lived?' Macrae said.

'Difficult to say. Some people . . . ' he glanced at Silver, 'have thicker skulls than others. But he was probably brain dead some time before his heart stopped.'

One of the Forensic team came into the room with a monkey wrench in a protective plastic bag. 'Found it in the garden.'

Macrae pointed to it and Dr Willey shrugged. 'The pathologist will tell you. It looks heavy enough.'

Macrae said, 'All right, laddie, tag it.' Then, 'You traced the wife yet?'

'Still not back,' Silver said. 'At least that's what her maid says.'

There was a commotion downstairs, voices were raised. Macrae and Silver moved towards the bedroom door. A man was climbing the staircase as though it was the north face of the Eiger. He climbed very slowly, one step after another. He was dressed in a black suit and waistcoat with a white shirt and black tie. He was one of the oldest human beings Silver had ever seen and the effort of climbing was taking all his strength and concentration. He was painfully thin and his skin had shrunk on to his bald skull as though he had been set out in a desert sun to dry.

Two large policemen were moving around him like sheep-dogs trying to turn him back. He simply ignored them and came implacably on. Finally, his breath rustling in his chest like leaves, he stopped in front of Macrae.

'You in charge?' he said, wheezily.

'Yes.'

'Name?'

'I'm Detective Superintendent Macrae. Who are you?'

'Her ladyship has asked me to inform you that she will see you now.'

Macrae looked at one of the uniformed PCs. 'What's he talking about?'

'Across the square, sir. Lady something—'

'Lady Hickson,' the old man said.

'Well . . . anyway . . . ' the policeman said. 'She's the one who phoned.'

'This way, sir,' the old man said.

Silver watched wide-eyed as the old man turned and went very slowly down the stairs again.

'Come on, laddie,' Macrae said to Silver.

They followed him out into the chilly night and across the short stretch of gravel which was all the square really was and found themselves being ushered into a house opposite.

'Kindly follow me,' the old gentleman said.

They followed him up an uncarpeted staircase to a sitting room on the first floor, their steps echoing hollowly through the house. As Silver trailed after them he noticed that the downstairs rooms were bare.

The old man paused and said to Macrae, 'Please bear in mind, sir, that her ladyship is no longer young.' He opened the door and announced: 'Detective Superintendent Macrae . . . and . . . assistant.'

Macrae and Silver found themselves in a room that might have been a film set for a house in the nineteen fifties. It was L-shaped and elegant with beautiful ceiling mouldings and had two long windows overlooking the square. At one end was a fireplace in which burned the kind of feeble, single-bar electric fire that was now only to be found on junk stalls in street markets. There was a bed in one corner, and a scrap-screen hiding a washbasin. There was a large Zenith radio-gram with automatic record changer which dominated one wall and next to it a small 12-inch TV set which might have been built by James Logie Baird himself.

There were piles of newspapers and magazines. Silver thought they must run into thousands. They covered tables and chairs and stood in neat piles on the floor reaching to knee-height. As he picked his way through this maze he noticed that the top copy of *The Times* on one pile was dated 1973.

By the window was a large chair under a reading lamp. In the chair was a woman so tiny that her feet did not touch the ground. She was dressed in a black, high-necked frock and had a worn rug of Black Watch tartan wrapped around her legs. Her grey hair was so thin that her pink scalp showed through it and her eyes had taken on the blue-mauve colour of extreme age. But they were bright and set in a heavily made-up face. Silver was reminded instantly of a bird. Beside her was a pair of powerful Zeiss binoculars on a mahogany stand.

Lady Hickson raised a small beringed hand in greeting. 'Would you gentlemen like a glass of whisky and a biscuit?' Her voice was surprisingly strong for such a frail body. When they refused she said, 'Thank you, Hay, you may go to bed now. I shan't want you again tonight.'

'Thank you, madam. Good-night, madam.' Hay gave a short bow and closed the door behind him.

She turned to Macrae and said in a chirpy voice, 'He won't, you know. Not until you've gone. Always the same. He's getting on a bit but a stickler for form. Now, what can I do for you?'

Silver had never seen Macrae deal with the aristocracy before and wondered how his anarchic character would display itself.

'You can tell us why you wanted to see us, your ladyship.' His voice was not disrespectful, it was not anything. Just neutral.

'You first,' Lady Hickson said, as though they were telling stories in the dorm at night. 'What's happened over there? A murder?' Her eys glittered and the years suddenly seemed to fall away.

'I'm afraid that's right, ma'am,' Macrae said.

'Good. Excellent. I said that to Hay but he gave me one of his looks. He doesn't approve of these, you know.' She indicated the binoculars. 'They were Dommie's. Dominic. My son. He died in the D-Day landings. They found these among his things.

'Hay thinks only the lower classes stick their noses into other people's business. It's the same with the furniture.

31

We've sold it room by room. No retirement plan, you see. Beating the Retreat, so to speak, to the first floor. I say, what does it matter? I can't use all the rooms anyway. But he hates to talk about it. He's a terrible snob. I've told him so a hundred times. Butlers always are. Not that he's a real butler, of course. Not properly trained. He was Daddy's servant in the war. After Daddy was killed at Ypres he came to us. I was only a little girl at the time.'

For a moment Silver was too nonplussed to take in what the old lady was saying. When she had said the war he had instantly thought of World War II. But it wasn't. It was the Great War. His mind made a quick calculation: if Mr Hay had been sixteen or so when the war started he would now be over ninety. Which made Lady Hickson over eighty. Silver tucked away the phrase 'getting on a bit' – which she had applied to Hay – for Zoe. She'd love it.

'People watch ships through telescopes,' Lady Hickson was saying. 'I watch people through these. I watch life. I can remember this square after the war. There was a pub on the corner. Now it's all changed. I've seen it change. Watched it all these years. Then my eyes grew a bit weak so I made Hay look for these binoculars. Can't tell you what a difference they've made. I like to look at the cars too. Lots of Porsches in the square. They say they're a frightful price. I had a sports car once. My husband Bertie gave it to me. Christmas nineteen thirty-eight. All wrapped up in Christmas paper with a big red Santa on the engine. MG. They don't make them any more. Not proper ones, anyway. So there *was* a murder? That man Healey?'

'That's right.'

'I thought he'd come to a sticky end.'

'Why?'

'Too much money. Too many girls.'

'May I ask how you know that, your ladyship?' Silver said, hearing himself adopt a kind of whining bended-knee tone and hating himself.

'I've watched him. Drives a pink Rolls Royce with his initials on the number plate. I think the Americans call them vanity plates. That's what he was, I should think. Rather vain. And insecure. I always say if you know who you are you don't need your initials on the car. You know them, don't you?'

She laughed brightly and Macrae nodded. 'Tell us about the girls,' he said.

'Rather young, if you ask me.'

'School-girls? That young?'

'Well . . . '

'He could have daughters,' Silver said.

She gave a contemptuous snort. 'And they could be nieces or cousins or family friends. Only I don't think so. D'you know what I think, Superintendent?'

'What do you think, ma'am?'

'Hanky panky.'

'Hanky panky?'

'You're a grown man, you know what I mean.'

'Have you any evidence for that, your ladyship?' Silver said. 'I mean did you see any . . . hanky panky through the binoculars.'

She gave him a withering look. 'I don't watch that sort of thing. Even if I'd seen it I wouldn't have watched it, if you know what I mean.'

'So there were girls,' Macrae said. 'What about today?'

'Well, it was earlier. I suppose between six and seven. I'd had a little sleep. You'll find that as you get less young you need a little nap every now and then. And Hay had brought me an egg. He doesn't have to, you know. I have biscuits and things and Meals-on-Wheels comes every other day. And there isn't really very much of me to—'

'Today,' Macrae said. 'Were there girls?'

'Just one. I'd had my egg. Hay knows just how I like them. Soft but not runny—'

'And you saw this girl . . . ' Macrae said, gently.

This was something else he'd have for Zoe, Silver thought: Macrae the gentle giant. He'd never seen him play this role before.

'Yes, she came running out of the house and forgot to close the door. She ran off down to the King's Road and went round the corner.'

'And this was some time between six and seven?' Macrae said.

'About then. Just after I'd had my egg.'

Silver noted it in his book.

'What was she like, this girl?' Macrae said. 'Very young?'

'Well, everyone seems rather young to me now, don't you know. But not a school-girl. Not that young. Not a pigtail or anything like that.'

Silver wondered how many schoolgirls wore pigtails these days. He'd have to ask Zoe.

'How was she dressed?' Macrae said.

'In slacks and a blouse and high-heeled shoes. Very high-heeled. Not much good for running in, I shouldn't have thought. And blonde hair. I noticed that first. Blonde hair and a black blouse and white slacks. Oh, and carrying a bag.'

'What sort of bag?'

'It looked like one of those you get at airports only bigger.'

'Shoulder bag?'

'She was carrying it in her hand and when she ran she was all lopsided.'

'The bag.'

'That's right. It made her lopsided. Well, I suppose it would, wouldn't it?'

'What made you phone for the police?' Silver said.

'The door, of course.'

'The door?'

'Young man, I don't know if you can leave doors open in your neighbourhood but we can't here. You've seen the bars on the windows. Highest robbery area in London. You should read the papers. Anyway, I watched the door. No one came out. It stood open and I thought: that's strange, we don't leave our doors open in this square. And after half an hour some youths came and stood there and looked in the door. I don't have to tell *you* what the young are like today, Superintendent.'

'No, ma'am.'

'Not all of them, of course. But the football supporters!'

'Were these football supporters?' Silver asked.

She gave him another of her looks and ignored the question.

'They hung about the door for a while and then went away. Not far away. Just to the end of the square. I watched them. They stood talking and looking at the house. You could see what was in their minds. So I called Hay and told him to telephone the police.'

'I'm glad you did,' Macrae said. 'If everyone was like you there'd be a drop in the crime rate.'

'That's what I said to Hay. But he thinks it's poking my nose in.'

After half an hour they left. Hay was asleep in a chair on the landing, head against the wall, mouth open. They tiptoed past so as not to wake him but he must have heard, for he stood up with a movement that sent the chair scraping backwards on the boards. He pushed past them and led them from the house, his old legs going stiffly down the stairs.

At the door, Macrae said, 'Her ladyship's husband, who was he?'

Mr Hay looked at him in surprise. 'General Sir Albert Hickson,' he said.

Silver realised the butler felt they should have known that.

Chapter 6

The building still had an old sign on it: MR MAGIC – GAMES.
But no games had been made in it or sold from it for many
years. It was in an industrial park on the edge of London
and had been vacant for a long time.

The area was called an industrial park because 'park' was
a buzz-word but this one was an old-style industrial estate,
with slab-sided brick buildings and ill-lit streets, graffiti and
used condoms.

Seedy. Run-down.

Now, at just after midnight, lights were on in the upper
windows of MR MAGIC. The top floor was a single large room.
In it was a glass cubicle where a foreman had once sat.
Against one wall were six wooden stalls. In each stall was a
desk. On each desk was a telephone. At each telephone was
a girl in her late teens or early twenties.

This was the office of the Xxxtasy chatline. In the glassed-
in cubicle sat the supervisor, a tacky blonde called Lex.
She was in her thirties with a face like plastic and a
skinny body.

The uncarpeted, uncurtained, unswept room hummed with
the noise of low voices in conversation. In the last stall sat a
girl named Barbara. She was twenty-one, dark, and would
have been attractive but for a bad skin. She had started work
at Xxxtasy three days before and had still not got used to the
stream of low-voiced filth that came out of the ear-piece of
her phone.

It rang now.

She said: 'Hello, Xxxtasy. This call is costing 44p a minute,

36

and 33p a minute off-peak. My name is Barbara. What would you like to talk about?'

There was a long silence.

'Hello, caller? Are you there?'

The voice was low and scarcely audible at first. 'Barbara?'

'This is Barbara. What would you like to talk about?'

'You don't sound like Barbara.'

'Oh?'

'I talked to Barbara yesterday.'

She felt her stomach clench.

'Who is that?' she said.

'You'd know if you were Barbara.'

'Is that Darth Vader?'

She heard a soft giggle.

'If you are Darth Vader then I remember you from yesterday.'

'Black Knight,' he said.

'Sorry?'

'My name is Black Knight.'

'I see . . . All right, Black Knight, what would you like to talk about?'

'You know what I want to talk about.'

'We are not permitted to talk about sex.'

'Oh yeah? I know you *have* to say that. But let's not bullshit about. OK?'

Barbara turned and signalled to Lex in the office. Lex picked up her phone and plugged straight into Barbara's conversation.

'What are you wearing, Barbara?' the voice said.

Barbara was wearing jeans, a T-shirt and trainers on her feet, but all the girls had been told what to say when they started work. She said, 'I'm wearing a see-through blouse and a G-string. Black fishnet stockings. Spike-heel pumps.'

'I'm wearing a shirt,' the voice said. 'Nothing else. You know what I've got in my hand?'

'I'm sorry but we can't . . . '

Lex was standing over her and hissed into her free ear.

'You'll bloody well talk about anything he wants, you silly little bitch. You keep him talking or you don't get your wages.'

'It's not what you think,' Black Knight said. 'I'll get to *that* later. I'm not forgetting *that*. No, it's something else. Something hard but cold. Something black and shiny. Something that smells of oil. I'm rubbing it up and down . . . up and down . . . '

Lex whispered fiercely, 'Talk to him. Tell him to enjoy himself. Tell him this is what you're here for. To help him enjoy himself!'

'Are you having a good time?' Barbara said, her voice wavering slightly.

'Yeah. A good time. You know what the Black Knight does?'

'No. I don't.'

'He's a symbol, see. Just like the White Knight. For forces. Forces inside everyone. People think the White Knight rights wrongs. But there're all kinds of wrongs. There ain't only one justice. You still there, Barbara?'

'Yes, Black Knight. Tell me about yourself. What turns you on?'

'You turn me on, sweetheart. Your voice turns me on. Your see-through blouse turns me on. Talking on this telephone turns me on. This thing in my hand turns me on. I'm going to use it, Barbara. I told you, didn't I?'

'Yes. You told me.'

She closed the mouthpiece and said to Lex, 'He's talking about it again! I'm scared.'

'They never mean it. It's only their fantasies. Don't let him hang up! Talk to him!'

When she'd got the job they'd told Barbara that Xxxtasy got 60 per cent of all the money from the calls so the longer they spoke the better.

'It's a gun, isn't it, Black Knight? The one you were telling me about yesterday.'

'Yes, Barbara. It's a gun. You know how I got it?'

'Tell me how you got it, Black Knight.'

'I found it.'

'Where?'

'On Wimbledon Common. You know why I was on Wimbledon Common?'

'Tell me, Black Knight.'

' 'Cause that's where women walk their dogs. Housewives. You know about housewives?'

'What about them?'

'They're frustrated, aren't they?' His voice was getting stronger now and he was talking more quickly. 'Stands to reason. Their husbands go off to work. No time in the morning, too tired of an evening when they get home. Don't you think?'

'I think you're right, Black Knight.'

'So I go to the Common to watch them. Sometimes I show them, you know?'

'Show them what?' she said in an unguarded moment.

'Guess.'

'Oh. Yeah. I understand.'

'I'd like to show you one day.'

'I'd like you to, Black Knight.' She felt her gorge rise, but Lex was still hovering.

Now Lex said, 'That's good. Keep him going.' Then she went back to her office to tune into the other conversations, to check that they too were going all right.

'So anyway, did you know there was a golf course there?'

'No.'

'Right on the Common. I used to pick up balls, sell them to the clubhouse. Easy money. All you needed was a stick to poke into the bushes. So one day I saw this box. Cardboard. But inside was a small black plastic bag. And inside that . . . you guess?'

'The gun?'

'That's right. The gun. Wrapped in a yellow duster. All oily. And another plastic bag with the bullets. Thirty bullets.'

39

There was a pause then he said, 'Listen . . . '
She listened.
Click . . . click . . .
'You hear that?'
'Yes, Black Knight.'
'That was me pulling the trigger. If there had been bullets in it you'd have been dead. Shot down the telephone line. Wouldn't that be amazing?'
She felt afraid again.
'I haven't killed anyone yet,' he said. 'But I'm going to. Two people. I know their names. I know where they live. A man and a woman. They're not married, but they live together and have sex together and they do things together. I know all about them. And I'm going to do things with them . . . Oh yes, with them . . . First I'm going to . . . going to . . . '
She hung up suddenly and sat quite still for a moment.
Lex was looking the other way, listening to someone else's call.
Barbara's phone rang again. She lifted the receiver. 'Hello. Xxxtasy. This call is costing 44p a minute and 33p a minute off-peak. My name is Barbara. What do you want to talk about?'
A different voice said, 'My name is Harry. I'm fifty-two years old and I'd like to take a bottle and—'
She put the receiver against her cheek so she could not hear what he wanted to do with the bottle.

Chapter 7

Silver surreptitiously raised his arm and sniffed at his black leather jacket. He thought he could still smell the sickly sweet odour of the morgue; a mixture of formaldehyde, antiseptic and soap.

He and Macrae and Mrs Robson Healey had just returned from formally identifying her husband's body and were in her apartment in a block of flats at the top of Hampstead Heath which, on this clear spring day, gave a view over London.

The apartment was obviously that of a wealthy woman yet it had no personality. It was the kind you ordered from Harrods, Silver thought. Catalogue number so-and-so. Furniture and fittings for one London apartment. State preferred colour.

And Mrs Healey herself looked as though she had come out of a catalogue. She was beautifully dressed in black. She might have been a model from the nineteen sixties. And although she must have been in her mid to late forties, she still had the body of a younger woman.

She had a pale skin, large brown eyes set wide apart and black hair drawn back. She was tall with good legs and she was wearing a pair of black high-heeled patent leather pumps.

She had a kind of icy remoteness that tantalised Silver and had retained it throughout the ordeal of identifying her husband's body and in the car coming back.

Now she said, 'I suppose you'll want to ask me questions.' The voice was hard and the accent patrician.

'Yes,' Macrae said.

41

She indicated a couple of overstuffed button-backed chairs and Macrae and Silver sat down gingerly.

'First of all,' Macrae said, 'I'd like to get a picture of your husband.'

She had perched on the arm of a chair. Her body-language was telling them to keep it brief.

'Surely, Inspector, you could get that out of any newspaper library.'

Macrae's face darkened. Silver knew he would hate being called Inspector.

To ease the tension, Silver said, 'One doesn't want to believe everything one reads in the papers.'

Mrs Healey smiled palely at him. Macrae glared.

'We'd like you to tell us,' Macrae said.

'He was in shipping, what more can I say?'

Macrae swung his heavy head away, then back to look at her and said, 'We can take as long as we need. This is what we're paid to do.'

She rose and lit a cigarette and walked to the big picture-window.

'Have you heard from your daughter yet?' Silver said.

'Not yet. I told you, Rachel's practically a hermit. She lives with this . . . with a young man called Nihill in the middle of nowhere. I have to leave messages at the local post office.'

'She knows about her father?'

'Yes, we spoke on the phone.'

'Were they close? Rachel and her father?'

'No, not really.'

'Let's get back to your husband. When were you married?'

'In nineteen sixty-five.'

'How old were you then?'

She turned and said, in a frozen voice, 'Is all this absolutely necessary? I mean these personal details? I think I should have my lawyer with me.'

'Murder is personal,' Macrae said. 'About the most personal thing that can happen to you. And if you want your lawyer why don't you phone him?'

42

She stared at him for a moment but made no move. Then she threw herself down in a chair and said aggressively, 'I was twenty at the time, which makes me forty-five now. Is that what you wanted to know?'

'Only if you think it matters.'

'We moved in different worlds. He was the son of a widow who worked in a factory. My father was a Crown Court judge.'

'How did you meet him?' Silver said.

'He owned a charter yacht in the Med. I went down to Antibes with a group and we hired the yacht. He skippered it. We were at sea for a week.'

'And?'

'We had an affair. I stayed down there for a couple of months.'

'And you were married soon afterwards?'

'I was pregnant. It was before abortion on demand.'

'That was Rachel.'

'Yes.'

'Any other children?'

'No.'

'What happened then?' Macrae asked.

'He went onwards and upwards. He'd started with dredgers but then he went into tankers and container ships. I can't tell you much about the business because he never discussed it with me.'

Macrae suddenly changed the subject. 'When were you divorced?'

'We've never been divorced.'

Macrae frowned and looked at his notes.

'People think we were. It's even been in the papers, you know the gossip columns. But we were legally separated. That's how he wanted it.'

'When was that?'

'In nineteen eighty-three. And if you're going to ask me why, my response is that the marriage had broken down.'

'Breakdowns are caused by a lot of things,' Macrae said, with feeling. 'Other women, drink, money, cruelty . . . '

'You sound like something of an expert.'

Silver waited for Macrae to react but all he said was, 'We see a lot of it in our business.'

She remained silent.

Macrae suddenly said, 'Where were you last night?'

'I have a cottage in Surrey. I was there.'

'Whereabouts?' Silver asked, his pen raised.

She gave him the address.

'Do you go down every weekend?'

'Mostly. And sometimes during the week for a night or two.'

'Is there anyone there who saw you?'

'Why?'

'To corroborate that you *were* there.'

'But I've told you I was.'

'Now we need someone else to tell us.'

'But for God's sake, you don't think . . . ' She did not finish the sentence.

Macrae smiled at her. It was not a pretty sight.

'Mrs Healey, a woman was seen running from the house yesterday evening about the time the murder was committed.'

Her eyes grew wide with apprehension. 'Well, it wasn't me, Inspector. I swear to you it wasn't me.'

'I'm sure you mean that, Mrs Healey. But that's no proof. And by the way I'm a Detective Superintendent not an Inspector. A small thing, but we all have our pride. Now, where were you exactly and do you have anyone who can support your story?'

Going back to Cannon Row in the car Macrae said to Silver, 'Rough trade. That's what she liked. Only it got complicated. Rough trade allied with money always does.' He looked down at his notebook at the name they had squeezed out of a reluctant Mrs Healey. 'Charles Harris,' he read.

'Weyford Marina, Surrey.' Then, 'I'll want you tomorrow, Eddie.'

'Come on!' Eddie was shouting through the windscreen at an ancient Austin which was moving sedately down Haverstock Hill at seven miles an hour. 'Get over!'

'Are you listening, Eddie?'

'I'm listening, guv'nor. Only that new Deputy Commander won't like it.'

'Who? Scales? To hell with him. You do as I say.'

'Right, guv'nor. Absolutely.'

Chapter 8

'Nice to see you, George,' the Deputy Commander said as Macrae entered his office. 'I've been wanting to meet you.'

He came round his desk and offered his hand. Macrae took it grudgingly.

'Heard all about you, of course. Who hasn't? The great thief taker.' He indicated a chair.

Macrae settled his bulk and the Deputy Commander went back to his own chair. He was of medium height with a narrow face. He was going prematurely bald and his thin hair was combed carefully across his skull. Macrae estimated that he was seven or eight years younger than himself.

'Your reputation's gone before you. The Murder Squad. The Flying Squad. The cutting edge, George.'

Macrae had seen Kenneth Scales for the first time the week before at a do in Scotland Yard, which was just over the road from Cannon Row police station. Freddie Pender, a desk sergeant Macrae had known for many years, was taking early retirement and Scales had made the speech. Scales had never met Pender and his unctuous words – more like a memorial service than a send-off – had embarrassed everyone including Pender himself who had rubbed his hands and shuffled his feet.

Macrae had had the word down the pipeline that Scales was coming to Cannon Row and had been prepared to hate him sight unseen. The speech had simply confirmed it.

'Coffee, George?'

'No thank you—' There was the slightest hestitation and then Macrae added the word, 'Sir'. He took out a packet of thin panatellas and was about to light one when he caught Scale's look and noticed, for the first time, a no-smoking sign on the wall behind him. He stuffed the packet back into his pocket.

'How're things going, George?'

'All right.'

'Good. Good.'

His accent jarred on Macrae. They said he'd been to university. Taken a degree in law. If that was the case, what did he want in the police? Why wasn't he a lawyer? Macrae had enough to put up with, what with Silver and his bloody university degree.

'I just wanted a little chat.'

'What about?'

'This and that. Get acquainted. I mean we're going to be working at the sharp end, George. Just as well to know each other.'

He leaned back in his chair and put his feet on the desk.

'D'you know why I was sent here?'

Macrae opened his mouth and closed it. He had taken himself firmly in hand before the interview. No fuck-ups he'd said to himself. No bullshit. He reminded himself of what Wilson was always telling him about promotion. Well, with Susan's trip to pay off and Mandy yelling for more money he'd have to think about that.

'I'm the new broom,' Scales said. The narrow face crinkled into a smile but the china blue eyes remained cold. 'I'm one of the chaps who has to pull the Met kicking and screaming into the next century.'

Macrae's big bull-like head fell forward slightly. 'In what way, sir?'

'I was hoping you'd ask me that.' Scales picked up a ball-point pen and began to click the little button on the side of it. Click . . . click . . .

He began to talk, slowly at first then with growing eloquence. He talked about computers; about computerisation on a vast scale. He used different words like interface

47

and synergy, cost-effectiveness and man management, then went on to the new structure of the Force. He spoke about the eight areas of London – the Area Major Incident Pool – and their organisation and re-organisation and re-re-organisation.

Click . . . click . . . went the pen.

And as he talked a glow came into his eyes. They shone with boyish sincerity.

He spoke of new attitudes to the public, of 'user friendly' police stations, of waiting rooms with carpets on the floors and pot plants, of being 'people-orientated'. He used words like parameter, and extrapolate . . . until it became obvious to Macrae that the copper on the beat had been replaced on Scales's mind by mainframes and megabytes and retrieval systems.

But all the while he nodded and Scales took his nodding for enthusiastic agreement, for he finally said, 'You should take a course, George.'

'In what?'

'Computer science.'

Macrae blinked. 'I don't think that's for me, sir.'

'Don't underestimate yourself. You're not too old. And I could help. I mean I could start you off.' Zeal shone from his eyes and Macrae's mind went back to his childhood on the banks of the Findhorn River in Scotland when a friend of his father's in the Free Presbyterian Church had spoken to him about God and the after-life. He had looked and sounded like Kenneth Scales.

'Anyway, think about it,' Scales said, bringing himself up short, as though realising he might have overdone the sincerity.

He gave the pen a few swift clicks and said, 'Now there are one or two other things, George.' But before he could start his wristwatch went 'Bleep! Bleep!' He pressed the reset button. 'I've spoken to Mr Wilson about this but I thought I'd mention it to you too. I want you to watch the DIs and the sergeants. All those boozy lunches. That's all over, George. And let me know of anyone keeping a bottle in his desk.'

Scales rose and Macrae rose with him. 'Is that all?'

'Yes, that's all, George. Except for one thing.'

Macrae, who had been halfway to the door, stopped and turned.

'You still use a driver.'

Macrae did not respond.

'Twyford, isn't it?'

'Aye. Eddie.'

'I'm sure you'll understand that's got to stop. It's part of the old money-no-object policing. You drive yourself now. Anyway, it's faster to go by tube and tubes are free for police officers.'

'Anything else?' Macrae's voice was dangerously controlled.

'That's all for now. Nice to have met the great thief taker at last.'

He put his hand on Macrae's shoulder. 'Don't forget about the computer course. It'll make your record look so much better.'

Macrae found himself out in the corridor. Silver was coming out of the incident room.

Macrae snarled, 'What's synergy mean?'

'Don't know, guv'nor.'

'Well go and find out and tell me in the Chief Super's office . . . and bring that bottle of Scotch from my desk . . . and two glasses . . .'

Detective Chief Superintendent Leslie Wilson watched Macrae come into his office and close the door behind him. George always made him feel uneasy. Sometimes worse.

'It's not on, laddie!' Macrae said. 'It's not bloody on!'

'What's not on, George?'

'You know what.'

'Scales?'

'Aye, Scales.'

Wilson had been waiting for this and not with any enthusiasm. Long ago, on a holiday in Spain, he had gone to a bullfight. Now he was reminded of that; putting Macrae into a room with Scales was like putting a bull into the ring with a matador.

'What'd he say, George?'

'I couldn't understand half of it. He's round the bloody twist. All he thinks about is computers. What he really wants is one bloody great computer with him telling it what to do in Bayswater and Greenwich and God knows where. I tell you, Les, I'm not standing for him.'

'It isn't a question of not standing for him. He's the boss. What he says goes.'

'You know what he said to me? He said he wanted me to do a course in computers.'

Wilson, who had earned the nickname 'Shifty' because of his habit of never allowing his eyes to rest on anyone or anything for more than a split second, covered the lower part of his foxy face and said, 'And what did you say, George?'

'I said I didn't think it was quite me.'

'And what did he say?'

Macrae gave it in Scales's accent. 'He said, don't underestimate yourself, George. You're not too old. Kept on calling me George and clicking his bloody pen!'

Silver came in carrying a bottle of whisky and two glasses. Wilson's pale face went paler. 'What the hell are you up to, Sergeant?'

Macrae reached for the bottle and glasses. 'I told him to bring them in.' He turned to Silver. 'Well?'

'Combined or co-ordinated action,' Silver said. 'As in working together.'

Macrae turned away and Silver left the room. Wilson was too concerned about the whisky to have registered the exchange. 'Christ, George, you must be out of your head. Scales is paranoid about liquor.'

'Aye, he told me.' Macrae poured two fingers into a glass

and was about to pour a second shot when Wilson put his hand up. 'Not for me, George.'

'You're not feared of that wee pimple are you?' In his anger Macrae's childhood accent was taking over.

'Of course not,' Wilson said. He tapped his stomach. 'The doc thinks it's an ulcer.'

Macrae sat down, overflowing a small straight-backed chair, and sipped morosely at his drink. 'Les, he's just a bloody kid. Can't be more than thirty-five.'

'What else did he talk about?'

'Boozy lunches.'

'I said so.'

'And Eddie.'

'Aah. You can't say I didn't warn you.'

'Listen, Eddie's been driving me ever since the old Murder Squad days. No one knows the routes better. Saves us hours. According to you saving money's everything. And time's money.'

'Can't help it. I let you get away with that. Scales isn't going to.'

'Fuck Scales. You know as well as I do that Eddie would've been out on early retirement years ago if it hadn't been for me. I got him tucked away in that filing job.'

'You can argue as much as you like but—'

'Oh, for Christ's sake, Les . . . '

The two men had known each other since they were coppers on the beat, had watched each other's backs, had spent Christmases together and gone on holidays together. Now they sat in an uneasy silence. Both were thinking the same thoughts. If Macrae's personality had been different, he would have been sitting behind the Deputy Commander's desk. Instead he didn't even have Wilson's rank.

'Aah . . . to hell with it,' Macrae said and poured himself another drink.

'Did he talk about promotion?'

'Aye. He thinks a computer course would work wonders. Well, he can stuff that.'

'Did he talk about the Healey investigation?'

'Not a word. Murder's not his speed. I checked his background. His experience at senior level has been in communications, complaints, training. Steering committees. And courses. Every bloody course you can think of. Twelve months as an inspector in Thames Valley then back to the Met. I bet you he's never even made an arrest. And he talks about the "sharp end" . . . "the cutting edge" . . . !'

Wilson's eyes flicked nervously round the room as though he expected to see Scales standing in a corner listening.

'Don't underestimate him. He's a clever lad so they say. Anyway, what gives?'

Macrae filled him in on what they'd found out so far.

'What about this girl the old lady saw? The one running from his house?'

'Could have been a tart,' Macrae said. 'The old lady said there were a lot of female visitors. I'll see Rambo about her.'

'You still using him?'

'From time to time.'

'Watch him, George, I don't trust him.'

'He's a criminal, Les. They're not supposed to be trust-worthy.'

Wilson waved his hand in the air. 'You know what I mean. Anyway, what else?'

'The ex-wife was out of town.'

'Alibi?'

'She gave us a name but we had to squeeze her for it. There's also a daughter in the West Country. We're going to see her.'

'By train, George.'

Macrae screwed back the top of the bottle and picked up the glasses. 'They've got new drugs for ulcers now. You take them and you can drink what you like.'

'Put it under your jacket! Christ, if he saw you coming out of my office with—'

'All right, all right.'

Macrae went to his own office and flicked through the messages from the incident room. The post-mortem was scheduled for the following day, but it looked definite that the wrench was the murder weapon.

He picked up the phone and put through a call to Eddie Twyford in the clerks' office.

'Yes?' Eddie said.

They arranged for Eddie to pick him up in Battersea early in the morning.

'Can you tell me where we're going?'

'All over the bloody place. The West Country. Surrey. That'll do for starters.'

'Right, guv'nor. I'll be there.'

Eddie leaned back in his chair. The West Country. He wondered what it was like. He didn't trust the countryside.

Chapter 9

Silver was lucky to find a parking place outside his apartment.
The time was round 8.30 and the evening was cold. He let
himself into the communal hall on the ground floor, picked
up his post from the hall table – brown envelopes – and
was about to start up the stairs when he remembered
he hadn't signalled to Zoe. He stuffed the post into his
pocket, went back, rang two shorts and a long on his own
bell and then went up the stairs to the top floor maisonette.
He unlocked the three deadlocks, went in, relocked them,
threw the bolt.

'Leo?' Zoe called from upstairs.

'I'm back.'

He dropped his jacket and went up into the open-plan
living room/dining room/kitchen. The smell was wonderful.

'What are we having?'

'*Pollo al ajo.*'

'What?'

The noise was prodigious. Zoe had tremendous passions
and her passion this month was for Handel's *Alcina.*
Sutherland's voice was overpowering in the small kitchen-
ette.

Leo turned down the volume. 'What's pollo whatever?'

'Hello, darling, lovely to see you. That's what we say when
we come in from work. Not "What are we having?"'

'Hello, darling, lovely to see you. Get your clothes off.'

'That's my boy. Chicken with garlic. And speaking of
clothes, now or later?'

'Why don't we take a bottle of that Australian white to
bed and have our drinks there.'

54

'Naughty.'

'And then come back and eat and watch an old movie.'

'Leo, you have such wonderful ideas. Is this a kind of Jewish thing?'

'What?'

'Fucking and eating and eating and fucking.'

'Sure.'

They went down to the bedroom and took a bottle of cold white wine and drank it and made love and lay with their arms around each other and listened to their stomachs rumbling.

'Come on, let's eat,' Zoe said.

She put on a kimono that was quite transparent. 'Just in case there're seconds,' she said. 'Girl guides be prepared.'

'Don't push your luck. I've had quite a day.'

She had been asleep when he came in the previous night and now, as they ate, he told her about the murder from the beginning, including the bits about Mr Hay and Lady Hickson he'd stored up for her.

Then he told her what he knew about Macrae and Scales and about the whisky. 'He's got a built-in self-destruct mechanism.'

'Why do you stay with him then?'

'You sound like my mother.'

'That's a bit incestuous, isn't it?'

For a long time she had never wanted to hear anything against Macrae. Or about the police in general. That was because of what had happened to her. But she'd got over that, or at least she wasn't having nightmares any longer. Her neurosis had been replaced by ambition for him; the same ambition his mother nursed. Onward and upward with the Met.

'You can't just go on being Macrae's little boy.'

'No. But at the moment it suits me fine. He has more contacts in the criminal world than any other copper in the Force. Things happen around him.'

'They must happen around other people.'

'He's like a honey trap.'

'Leo, you've got your own life.'

They finished dinner and put on an old black and white movie and sat on the sofa. She curled up against him.

But he could not concentrate. How could he explain about Macrae? His thoughts went back to his own beginnings in the Force. It was only a few years ago but seemed like a lifetime.

'I solemnly and sincerely declare and affirm that I will well and truly serve our Sovereign Lady the Queen in the Office of Constable without favour or affection, malice or ill-will, and that I will, to the best of my power, cause the peace to be kept and preserved . . .'

That was the oath he had sworn at the Hendon Police College.

And that's what he'd done – caused the peace to be preserved. The Queen's peace. He loved that phrase. It sounded more Elizabethan than contemporary. The kind of phrase Raleigh or Drake might have used.

He remembered the section house in London where he had first lived as a probationer. He remembered the lectures on the possibility of contracting AIDS and hepatitis from prisoners and how the police were more worried about the latter than the former because just about every tart in London was a hepatitis carrier.

And he remembered the money.

Soon after he had passed out of college he was deluged with letters about money. They came from banks and credit agencies offering what seemed like limitless credit on easy terms. They said it was because he was trustworthy, because he was a policeman.

The other young cops were spending money as though it was going out of fashion. So did he. It was the first time in his life he had had a cheque book. His wallet was stuffed with credit cards. He bought sharp clothes and a car and went on holiday to Portugal.

And then all of a sudden he was getting different letters from the banks and the credit agencies and these weren't friendly at all.

This was soon after he had left the uniformed branch and gone into the CID. It was the first time he had met Macrae. They had been on a job near London Airport and Macrae had intercepted a message for him from a debt-collecting agency.

Macrae had taken him for a drink and said, 'Tell me about it, laddie.'

He'd told him.

Macrae had said, 'It's an offence in the police to get into debt. Give me your cheque book and your cards.'

Macrae had bent and broken up the credit cards and put the cheque book in his pocket. He'd told Silver to sell the car and put aside money to pay off his debts. He was as tough as hell. When Silver needed a new pair of socks or a pair of shoes he had to go to Macrae, who would tear out one cheque, make it out, and Silver would sign it.

In fourteen months he was in the black again and Macrae gave him back his cheque book.

There were no guns or knives involved. Macrae hadn't saved his life or done anything dramatic. But it was important. He would never forget. He owed him.

They were both almost asleep when the movie ended. 'You want anything?' Zoe said. He shook his head. 'Let's go to bed then.'

They went down the stairs to the bedroom on the floor below. Silver had flung his jacket down on a chair and it had slipped on to the rug. Zoe bent to pick it up and in doing so saw the letters sticking out of the pocket.

'Is this all the post?'

'Yeah. Only bills.'

'Gas. Electricity. Garage.' She handed them to him. Then she frowned at the last envelope. It was addressed to 'Zoe' and carried no stamp. She opened it but it was empty.

'There's writing on the back flap,' she said.

'What's it say?'

She held it to the light. 'B . . . A . . . no not A, O . . . L . . . T . . . O . . . P . . . BOLTOP. What's it mean, Leo?'

'No idea. Probably some intensive advertising campaign.'

'Nonsense.'

'They write something that doesn't make sense and try to intrigue you. We'll probably see it written on telephone poles and on the pavement.'

'I don't think so. I've never heard of it.'

'That doesn't make it wrong.'

'For God's sake, Leo, I work for an advertising agency *and I've never heard of it*! Anyway, why just "Zoe"? No address. No stamp. Someone stuck this through the letter-flap. Then one of the other flat-owners picked up all the envelopes after the post arrived and put them on the table. And this was with the others.'

'It might even have been on the table this morning,' Silver said. 'I never look at brown envelopes when I'm going out.'

'Nor do I.'

'BOLTOP . . . ' He shook his head.

'Leo, d'you think—?'

He knew what she was going to say because it happened so often. Her mood change was abrupt, as though the thoughts were just below the surface of her mind.

'Of course not. How the hell could he have put it through the letter-flap? He's still inside.'

'He could have given it to someone who was coming out.'

'But he doesn't know we're together. Doesn't even know where we live.'

'Jesus, Leo, you're supposed to be a detective! I know I'd have got the information if I wanted it.' She was angry now as well as showing fear. 'He couldn't . . . ?' She paused as though unwilling to continue the question.

'What?'

58

'Couldn't be out, could he?'

'No.'

'Are you sure?'

'Yes.'

'Leo, you've got to find out. You've got to make certain.'

'Sure.'

'Now. Pick up the phone. Ring someone.'

'Who, for God's sake?'

'The prison.'

'They'd never give me information like that over the phone. Not at this time of night.'

'You said you'd keep a check on him. You swore you would.'

'I did. And I will.'

'You swear?'

'Of course. I'll find out which gaol and how much longer he has to serve. Every detail.'

'What if he's out?'

'He's not. He can't be.'

'Leo, what are we going to do when he does come out?'

'Don't worry. I'll keep an eye on him.' She turned away but he caught her hands. 'Listen, you can't let him ruin your life. These people are cowards. They only attack in the dark or lonely places. They're more afraid than you are. Specially after a prison sentence. He'll probably be broken anyway.'

'Oh God, I'm so scared.'

'Don't be. You needn't be. I'll look after you.'

In bed she clung to him like a child who has had a bad dream. He knew the dream. He had had it too: the shed, the knife, the blood on her naked belly, the man with his flies open.

And for the umpteenth time he questioned himself about her reason for living with him. Was it love? Or was it for protection. And if it was the latter, was that any basis for marriage?

* * *

The pub was lost in the wastes of Stockwell. It was called the Black Swan but no swans, black or white, had been seen in that part of London in living memory, so people had re-christened it the Mucky Duck. It was a survivor – just – of the formica fifties and a place of such unparalleled dreariness that Macrae sometimes met his contacts there. As far as he knew, no self-respecting villains ever darkened the doorway.

He met Rambo there a little after half past eight. They took their drinks to a table where the light was so dim that Rambo's pallor appeared deathly. Even in bright sunlight, as Macrae had frequently seen him, he did not look much better. He was a plump and unhealthy thirty-something and Macrae always felt that if he prodded him with the tip of a finger the indentation would remain for hours.

But the point about Rambo – whose real name was Julius – was that he was over six feet in height and weighed nearly three hundred pounds.

'Cheers,' he said, raising his glass.

Macrae grunted.

'How's the family, Mr Macrae?'

'All right.'

Rambo's father had been a clown in a small touring circus. He had wanted his son to follow in his footsteps but Rambo had started to grow early, had seen the writing on the wall for small circuses and large men, and instead had taken to writing other people's names on cheques. That was when he was seventeen. When he was nineteen he was nicked and given a suspended sentence. By the time he was in his late twenties he was into cheque fraud on a grand scale. He was stealing cheques and cheque cards – or paying others to steal them – and then cashing as much in one day as he could before throwing both away.

It was an energetic way to make a living. The maximum he could draw from any one bank then was fifty pounds, and out of that he had to pay the thief half. So it was a matter of quantity.

60

In order to hit as many banks in a day as he could meant meticulous planning. It also demanded stamina. His record was thirty-one between opening time at 9.30 a.m. and closing time at 3.30 p.m.

On the day he set his record he was still going flat out at 3.25 p.m. He'd just done all the banks in Hammersmith Broadway, running on his large, fat legs from one to the next, and had then moved to Chiswick.

With only a few minutes to go he hit a Midland and just made a Barclays as they were shutting the door. Blowing and puffing he went up to the nearest cashier, held out his cheque – and collapsed in a heap on the floor.

The manager called the ambulance service, was told it sounded like a heart attack and that he should loosen Rambo's clothing and cover him with a blanket. While they were doing this they found fourteen cheque books with their accompanying cheque cards as well as pockets stuffed with five-pound notes.

Macrae, who was doing a spell in the Fraud Squad, had interviewed Rambo in hospital.

'There's not much point in denying it, laddie, is there?' he'd said.

'No, Mr Macrae.'

So he'd pleaded guilty at his trial and gone down for two years. When he came out he was a changed man. The heart attack had scared him. He didn't go back into cheque fraud but with his contacts in the circus and the fact that circuses were going out of business every month or so he began to put together a string of girls – trapeze artistes, fire-eaters, bare-back riders, lion-tamers – that gave sex a completely new dimension.

The girls were often privy to important underworld information and sometimes he passed this on to Macrae; not for the money – he was doing well enough – but for reasons he could hardly understand himself.

Any psychologist would have understood them. Macrae had been the only person to visit him in hospital. Not the only police person but the only person – period. In his subconscious this fact had transmuted Macrae from copper into friend.

Macrae said, 'How's business?'

'Not bad, Mr Macrae, not bad. I think we've found a gap in the market.'

'How's Frenchy?'

'Taking her mum on a bus tour of Scotland. You want her to come over when she gets back?'

'I'll see.'

'She's got a soft spot for you, Mr Macrae.'

'Yeah . . . well . . . You're remembering what I said?'

'What was that?'

'Julius, you know bloody well.'

Macrae was one of the few people who called him Julius and he appreciated it.

'You mean about underage girls?'

'Of course I mean that.'

'I swear on my mother's grave.'

'You never had a mother.'

'Cross my heart.'

'Just you remember.'

'On my oath!'

Macrae said, 'Robson Healey. The name mean anything to you?'

'Only what I read in the papers. Shipping. Deceased.'

'Deceased is putting it mildly.'

Chapter 10

'Hello . . . this is Xxxtasy. Your call is costing 44p a minute and 33p a minute off-peak . . . My name is Barbara. What would you like to talk about?'

Ronnie kept silent. This was the moment that gave him the initial charge: the little pause before he spoke. It made him feel powerful.

'Barbara?' he said.

He could hear a sudden intake of breath. That was good.

'Barbara speaking.'

'Guess,' he said.

'I recognised your voice.'

'I'm in a phone booth near Victoria Station. There's every sort here. Blokes dressed up as girls, girls dressed up as blokes. You can get stoned for a couple of quid. You ever been stoned?'

She did not reply.

'I'd like us to get stoned together. I mean out of our skulls. So we were different people.'

'That'd be great,' Barbara said, trying to express warmth.

'Who'd you like to be?'

'Like to be?'

'If we were stoned.'

'I don't know. Who'd you like to be?'

'I am.'

'You are?'

'You know bloody well.'

'Black Knight.'

'Yeah.'

*Sideways and forward or forward and sideways but never in
a straight line . . . That was old Crowhurst. He'd made a chess
board and taught Ronnie. And then at Granton Ronnie had
played chess with one of the psychologists. And the guy had
asked him why he wanted to play chess – just like they asked
him why he wanted to do every bloody thing – and if he said
why the fuck do you want to know, they would say why do you
think we want to know, Ronnie? And so he'd said he found
chess cathartic. Cathartic. That had impressed the bastard.
But Barbara wouldn't know what it meant. Neither would his
mother . . .*

'Are you there, Black Knight?'

'I'm here. I've been watching them.'

'Who?'

'The two I told you about. I saw her tits. At the window.
She came to the window with nothing on. Exposing herself.
Small tits. I like them bigger.'

Barbara said, 'I see.' She still wasn't expert at this.

'It's like a massage.'

'What?'

'This conversation.'

'That's good.'

'Massages relax you. I want to be relaxed. Because pretty
soon, Barbara, I'm going to . . . guess . . . '

'I can't, Black Knight.'

'I want you to call me darling.'

'I'm sorry I—'

'I'll speak to your bloody supervisor! I'm paying for this,
remember!'

'There's no need,' she said quickly.

'Well call me darling then.'

'All right.'

'All right, darling.'

'All right . . . darling.'

'OK, so now I'll tell you. They don't know I've been
watching them. She walks around the room without clothes

64

Macrae had no option but to take it.

'We were just having a cup of coffee, George. Come in and join us.'

'I don't want to intrude,' Macrae said, but instantly followed her into the flat.

The big room had a bay window. The curtains were drawn and the room, with only two spotlights playing on a ficus and a kangaroo vine, was dim and cosy. The predominating colours were white and green. The room cut through the apartment to the rear where there was a pine dining suite. From the plates and glasses Macrae realised that they must have just finished dinner.

'Do you still take it black with sugar?' Linda said, pouring George a cup.

'Aye. Still the same.'

'Brandy?'

There were two large snifters on the coffee table.

'If you're having one,' he said.

She went to fetch a glass and Leitman said, 'Not a very nice night.'

'No.'

'Won't you sit down?'

Macrae didn't like being asked to sit down by some stranger in his ex-wife's flat. Instead he walked to the window, touched the dark green velvet curtains then turned and studied Leitman. There was nothing subtle about it, he studied him as though he was a suspect in a police line-up.

He saw a thin man with dark brown eyes and an aquiline face, greying hair and humour lines incised round his mouth. His accent was neutral. He was wearing a white polo-neck sweater, dark-blue corduroy trousers and white buckskin shoes. Macrae, who dressed formally, thought he looked like an actor and was ready to despise him.

The only thing going for Macrae was that Leitman was older than he was himself. He guessed he was in his late forties or early fifties.

As Macrae was examining him, Linda, at the far end of

the room, looked over the snifter of brandy she was pouring for Macrae and studied them both.

David was something new in her life. He had moved into the flat upstairs three months before and they had greeted each other on the communal staircase.

She was wary about the kind of relationship that arose between people who shared the same building. She had heard several stories of affairs that had started well but then, when over, had not been allowed to die naturally because the lovers lived too close to each other.

She had searched long and hard for this flat and it suited her. And even though she was lonely now that Susan had left the nest, she thought it a fair price to pay for an uncomplicated life.

So she had kept to herself. But so had David. He had made no move to expand on 'Good morning' or 'Good evening'.

He became something of a mystery to her. She had no idea what he did. He never wore a tie or a suit. And always seemed to be at home.

Two weeks before she had seen him at the local supermarket staring uncertainly at a shelf of cleansing powders. She greeted him, and he said, 'What does an automatic powder look like?'

'It's not the powder that's automatic,' she said, laughing, 'it's the machine.'

'Aha! They didn't tell me that.'

She pointed out a powder and went on her way. Later that Saturday there had been a knock on her door and he had asked for help.

His kitchen floor was awash with foam and water. 'I'm not much good with machines,' he had said, defensively.

She helped him mop up and had then shown him how to use the machine. He had given her a cup of coffee, they had talked, she had left.

The greetings on the stairs had been slightly warmer after that but that was all. Then, a few days ago, she had said, 'How's the washing machine?'

'Fine, if you like washing machines.'

Before she knew what she was doing she had said, 'Would you like to come in and have a meal some time?'

'I was just about to ask you if you'd come out to dinner with me.'

She thought his diplomacy was perfect.

'No truly,' he said, as though to dispel any such idea. 'Cross my heart.'

'Well, I asked you first.'

'I'd like that very much. On one condition, that you let me bring the wine.'

And so they had had dinner and he had told her briefly about himself. He had two grown-up children and been divorced for nearly three years. It was a background not unlike her own.

And then George had arrived.

Linda brought the brandy to Macrae who took it in his big fist.

'David's a writer,' she said. 'You may have seen his books.'

Macrae thought for a moment and then shook his head. 'Do you write under your own name?'

Leitman's mouth turned up in a small smile. 'Strangely enough, I do. It's L-e-i-t-man. My great-great-grandparents came from Leipzig. When I worked on the *Chronicle* they made me spell it Lightman. The other was too foreign.'

'The *Chronicle*? You'd have known the crime man then.'

'Norman Paston? I've known him for years.'

'George always likes to check up,' Linda said. 'He never takes anything at face value.'

'What sort of books do you write?' Macrae said.

'Police procedurals.'

'Police what?'

Leitman smiled again, as though he was sharing a joke with himself. 'Well, it's embarrassing to discuss my work with someone like you. Linda told me what and who you are.'

Linda thought he did not look embarrassed at all.

Macrae said, 'You mean like what sort of paper-clips we use. And Zebra Bravo calling Base . . . Roger over and out.'

'Not quite. I'm more interested in the policeman as a social animal living in an enclosed society.'

Macrae gave a harsh laugh. 'Enclosed society?'

Linda watched him nervously as he took half his brandy in a single gulp.

'The police always think they have their backs to the wall. Whatever they do doesn't seem to be right. It's given them a kind of inferiority complex.'

'*What?*'

'I don't mean individually, though one could probably make a case for that. But there's a kind of corporate personality. The miners have it too. A feeling that no one understands them; that everyone but their own kind is against them.'

'Where'd you get all this stuff?' Macrae said. 'Books?'

'And newspapers and television and my own observations. And I know a few ex-detectives who guide me.'

'Oh.'

'You see, George, he does his homework,' Linda said.

'You make it sound as though we're a kind of sub species,' Macrae said.

'You are in a way. Look at the statistics. A higher divorce rate than average. A higher alcoholism rate than average. A higher stress rate than average. More financial problems than average.'

Macrae thought for a moment, said nothing, then drained his glass and stood up.

Linda made no move to stop him.

'I'll be getting back to my enclosed society,' Macrae said, and nodded curtly at Leitman.

Linda came to the street door with him. She sensed that if she let him comment on David they'd have another row. So she quickly said, 'I had a letter from Susan last week. From Bali. She's having a lovely time and it's doing her good.' She opened the door. 'Good-night, George.'

Before he knew it he was standing on the front step and the door was closing behind him and the rain was coming down on his head.

When he got back home to Battersea he gave himself a large whisky and phoned Norman Paston on the *Chronicle*. They spoke briefly about the Healey killing. Paston, who often worked in a symbiotic relationship with George, had no information to offer.

Macrae said, 'Know a bloke called Leitman?'

'David Leitman? There was a David Leitman on the *Chronicle*. Nice man. Good writer. Why?'

'I met him.'

'I'm surprised you haven't read him. He writes police novels. Good ones too.'

'Why read about it when you're doing it all the bloody time?'

'That's the spirit, Georgie.'

He put down the phone, poured himself another whisky, turned on the TV, and watched the late news. There was a picture of Healey's house in Chelsea with police cars outside it. He saw Silver come out into the square. Then himself. He thought he looked old.

Police procedural!

He felt anger take hold of him. He wanted to comfort himself by sneering at Leitman for being a writer. But like all Scots he had respect for the written word and for the people who put it down on paper.

Chapter 11

Sometimes when the mood took her, or she 'had the fever' as Chris had put it, Rachel Nihill would blank out and paint all day and all night. In fine weather she painted outside in the forest; when it was cold or rainy, in the caravan. At night she painted by the light of an oil lamp. She would paint . . . and paint . . . in oils or poster paints or acrylic; on canvas or hardboard or paper . . . anything that came to hand.

She had just gone through such a spell, a feverish slice of time when days merged into nights and nights into days without her consciously realising the change. She was not even sure how long this 'fever' had lasted, nor how many paintings she had made or what their subjects were.

She stood outside under the grey morning sky and looked at the dense growth of oaks and beech trees and wild elder which surrounded her. This glade was so remote that she could hear no noise of traffic, could see no building or man-made artefact. All she could hear was the bell of Lexton church in the distance.

When she had first come here with Chris it had been winter and the forest a place of dark magic. She had been frightened.

Now she had become used to it. She belonged.

The caravan had once been owned by a real gyspy but it had fallen into decay. It had been Chris's idea that she should buy it. He had been excited by the prospect, which was not surprising since he was part gypsy himself.

He had refurbished it, painted the wood a dark reddish brown and had decorated it in true gypsy fashion with curlicues of green and gold. The interior matched. There were two bunks, a little dresser for china and pots and pans and a small wood-burning stove for heating and cooking. Everything was miniature. When it was finished Rachel had never seen anything so beautiful.

She had named it EREWHON. Chris had wanted to name it WANDERER but it was hers to name. He had made a poker-work nameplate which he had fixed near the door. They had bought a horse which she christened Nemo and they had wandered together along the narrow lanes of Somerset until they came to the Forest of Dean. He had grown up in similar countryside and was immediately at home. But the forest reminded Rachel of Victorian fairy tales about mad giants and witches and lost children.

Now, standing outside the caravan, as the breeze ruffled her long, flowing dress, she felt, for the first time since Chris had left her, that she could face the day. She told herself that this was a new start. She had her own life to lead, she need not be dependent on him or any man.

In the past few days she had gone through a . . . she searched for the word and found it . . . a catharsis. It had started with Chris's disappearance and ended in a spell of furious painting. Now she felt weak but calm.

Hesitantly she took a deep breath. There was no choking sensation, no blockage, no breathlessness. Her lungs were clear. If she was careful they might stay that way. She might even be able to think of what had happened to her father without getting the panicky feeling which always signalled another attack.

The day stretched ahead. She did not feel like painting – that was over for the time being – but she knew she would have to go through the work she had done. She would burn some paintings, as she always did, and keep one or two. But first she must put flowers on kitten's grave.

The glade in which the caravan stood was surrounded by wildflowers. There were bluebells and cowslips and wild geraniums.

She walked past the place where Nemo had been tethered

and began to pick the flowers. When she had collected a small bunch she walked deeper into the woods to the grave and placed them under the cross she had made of twigs.

And this was where Macrae and Silver found her.

They had left London before breakfast with Eddie Twyford driving the unmarked Ford. The journey had started badly. Macrae and Eddie had argued about the quickest way from Battersea to the M4. Macrae had won and they had become jammed in traffic near the river because of a burst water main. Then they had stopped for breakfast and Macrae had said that his poached egg was 'off' and had made a scene about it.

And now they were lost.

'For God's sake stop and let's look at the map,' Macrae said.

'I looked at it before we left, guv'nor.' Eddie peered at the forest with suspicious, uneasy eyes.

'I think we should have gone left about three miles back,' Macrae said.

'There was no sign, guv'nor. Nothing that said Lexton.'

They came to a village and Silver got out to ask the way.

'Straight on,' he said, proving Eddie right. Macrae's body language said he wasn't too happy about that. He sat hunched in his overcoat and hat as though travelling in an unheated car forty years ago.

They moved deeper into the forest. They were surrounded now by trees and undergrowth. Soon they entered the hamlet of Lexton, dominated by its church, the spire black against the grey sky.

There were a dozen houses, a pub, and a single shop. It was part post office, part supermarket and part hardware store. It also sold postcards, stationery, maps and guide books.

An elderly lady with blue-grey hair was furiously counting money behind the brass bars of the post office counter.

In reply to his question about Rachel Nihill she looked severely at him over half-lens spectacles and said, 'I am a

74

public servant. I cannot divulge information of the sort you require.'

She had an over-refined voice as though she had taken elocution lessons.

'All I want to do is talk to her,' Silver said.

'I'm sorry.'

She turned back to the small pile of notes and began counting again.

Silver pushed his warrant card on to the counter. She studied it for some seconds. 'A policeman!' Her eyes glinted and she ran her tongue over her lips. 'Oh well, that is indeed different. As far as I know, and it is only what I am informed – she and her husband are living on Old Beauty.'

'Old Beauty?'

'The old iron mine.'

She gave him directions, he bought a guide book, and came back to the car.

'It's not far, guv'nor. There's a mine. She's on the property somewhere. She comes up to the post office every day to check for mail and buy supplies. But she hasn't been up the last few days.'

'You want me to go down *there*?' Eddie asked, looking at a muddy, potholed track.

'For Christ's sake, if that's the way then take it!' Macrae said.

'I'd rather take the Old Kent Road in rush hour.'

'Come on, Eddie, get a move on.'

They bumped down the track for another half-mile and then Eddie stopped. His mouth had set in a tight line. Macrae said to Silver, 'How far now?'

'She said it wasn't more than a mile.'

Macrae said to Eddie, 'We'll walk. Turn the car round.'

'Where?'

'You'll find a place.'

They went on down the track passing an old brick chimney and the remains of the winding gear of an iron mine. The trees were in their new shiny leaves but neither took much

75

notice. Macrae walked with his eyes down to avoid the mud, Silver scanned the guide book.

'They've been mining iron here since before Roman times.'

Macrae did not reply.

'They stopped in 1945.'

Macrae grunted.

'I didn't know the word miner used only to refer to iron miners. Coal miners were called colliers.'

'Where'd you get all this guff?'

'Guide book. It says all those born outside the forest are regarded as foreigners.'

Macrae stopped and Silver caught up with him. They stood for a moment looking at Rachel Nihill. She was kneeling on the ground and looked small and very alone. She heard them and turned.

'Mrs Nihill?' Macrae said.

'Ms.'

'I'm Detective Superintendent Macrae. This is Sergeant Silver. We've come from London.' He held his warrant card out but she hardly glanced at it.

'I was putting some flowers on kitten's grave,' she said.

'I had a kitten once,' Silver said. 'It died too.'

'I suppose you've come about my father.'

She led them back to the caravan.

'Anything you could tell us would be helpful,' Macrae said.

She stood by the fire, her right hand cupping her left elbow. Silver was struck by the pose, especially in combination with the long flower-patterned dress. He looked at her closely. She was a plain young woman with mousey hair. Early twenties, he estimated. Small. Thin. In the clear light he could see that she had once had a problem with her skin.

'Would you like some coffee?'

Silver said, 'That'd be great.'

She gave them each a mug from the black metal pot that stood by the side of the fire. Silver thought it tasted of woodsmoke and chicory. She sat on the caravan steps.

'It's lovely,' Silver said, indicating the caravan. 'I've never seen one close-up before.'

'Chris did most of it.'

'Is that your husband?'

'You haven't come to talk about him, have you?'

Macrae always liked to find the reason for reluctance.

'We've come to talk about everyone: you, your mother, Chris – Christopher?'

'That's right.'

Silver made a note.

'And my father.'

'What?'

'You've come to talk about my father.'

'Aye. Your father, naturally.'

'Who told you I was here? My mother?'

'Of course.'

'The bitch.'

'Didn't you want us to know?' Silver said. He had been walking round the caravan, admiring it.

'I don't care what you know. I just don't like her interfering, that's all.'

'It's not her fault,' Macrae said. 'We asked her.'

'D'you mind if I go in?' Silver asked.

'Have you got a search warrant?'

'Have you got something to hide?' Macrae asked.

'Why do you want to go in?' she asked Silver.

'Well, it's lovely. I'd just like to see how you've done it up.'

She shrugged. 'OK.' She moved from the steps and adopted the same pose as before. She turned her pale-blue eyes on Silver – eyes that should have been lovely had she had colour in her face – and watched him as he went up the steps. 'Mind your head,' she said.

'Tell me about yourself,' Macrae said.

'Do I need a lawyer?'

'Do you think you do?'

She laughed dryly. 'You answer questions with questions.'

Macrae threw the dregs of his coffee on to the ground. 'That's why we're here. To ask questions.'

'But why me?'

'You're his wee girl. We're trying to get a picture of him. We know a bit about him, not much. There isn't a lot in the files.'

'He paid people to keep his name *out* of the papers.'

'You can't keep secrets from your own family. Or at least not completely, unless you work at it.'

'He did.'

'Who's the artist?' Silver said, coming down the steps.

'If you mean the paintings, then I did them.'

He smiled. 'What have you got against rabbits?'

Macrae was irritated at the interruption and went back to question her earlier statement. 'You mean he kept secrets from you? Or that he worked hard to keep them from the family?'

'Both.'

'In what way?'

'Look, I haven't lived with my family for years.'

'Doesn't matter.'

'All I ever wanted was to get away from them. I ran away from school once when I knew they were coming down for Parents' Day.'

'Where did you run to?'

'London. I caught a bus and spent the day there. My father was furious. He came down and threatened to sue the headmistress and the governors and God knows who else if it ever happened again.'

'Did it?'

'No.'

'Were you afraid of your father?'

'Yes. He was a bastard. He hurt people. He hurt my mother.'

'Are you sorry he's dead?' Silver broke in.

'I'm not sorry.'

'Are you pleased?'

'In a way.'

'You must have hated him.'

'I suppose so. All I ever wanted to do was get away from him. And from my mother too. May I ask you a question?'

'Go ahead,' Macrae said.

'Did you love your parents?'

His big head fell slightly forward in what Silver had described to Zoe as his 'minotaur' pose. He looked discomfited.

'I'm being honest with *you*,' she said.

'One of them,' Macrae said unwillingly. 'My mother.'

'In my class at school about sixty per cent of the girls disliked their parents.'

Macrae switched the subject. 'You say he hurt your mother: how?'

She began to walk slowly up and down on the far side of the stone fireplace. 'He was rude. He laughed at her. Sometimes he laughed at her posh accent. She's not all that bright. Sometimes he called her stupid.'

'But did he hit her?' Silver said.

'Not in front of me, but I heard them having rows occasionally. I saw bruises. She was often in tears.'

'What caused the rows?'

'His other women.'

'Did he always have other women?'

'I think so.'

'How old were you when they separated?'

'Fifteen. I was supposed to live with my mother. But I worked it so I spent the holidays on school trips. I think she was pleased and he was away a lot of the time. Then I came into a trust fund when I was eighteen. Not much but I could get along on my own. Do what I liked.'

'And this is what you like?' Silver said. 'Living in a gypsy caravan in a forest?'

'I didn't know it till I met Chris.'

'Tell us about him.'

'Why?'

79

'It helps us get a picture,' Macrae said.

'I was at art school.'

'He was taking art?'

'No. He was a . . . well, he was a carpenter. A cabinet-maker. He did some work in the house where I was lodging. We met that way.' She paused. 'He was the first person who was ever kind to me.'

'Did he know you had money?'

'I told him all about it. But you're wrong if you think that's . . . I mean it's not much money. He's part gypsy. He was restless. He wanted to travel, to wander. So I bought the caravan. He fixed it.'

She told them about their journey and how they had fetched up in the Forest of Dean.

'When did he split?' Silver said.

'A few days ago.'

'Why?'

'That's my business. Just say we had a disagreement. So he left and took Nemo.'

'Who's Nemo?'

'The horse.'

'Where did Chris come from originally?'

'Why?'

'We have to check on everyone.'

'I suppose so. Lympton in Wiltshire.'

'Do you have an address for him?'

She shook her head. 'He isn't the kind of person who has an address.'

Half an hour later they left. Silver felt guilty as they walked back up the track. He turned once and raised his hand. She looked so defenceless. It reminded him of a Victorian painting. 'A Forest Moment.' Something like that . . .

Rachel watched the two detectives until they were out of sight.

She was alone.

She said the phrase out loud: 'I am alone.'

Boarding school did not fit people for solitude, she thought. After school there had been art college and lodgings and then Chris. She had almost never been alone. Till now.

Only an hour or so before, she had stood by the open fireplace, which he had made with rounded boulders, watching the water come to the boil for coffee and had felt a sense of freedom and calm. But the visit by the two detectives had destroyed that.

The day stretched ahead and was less inviting than it had been. Freedom had its problems. She had wanted everything: happiness, Chris, the caravan, the forest . . . Now she only had the caravan and the forest.

Once, when she had expressed doubt about the length of the journey from Hampshire through the winding lanes, Chris had said she should think of it in terms of a mile at a time. If she thought of the whole journey she would never start.

This is what she would have to do with her time now. She must not think of the months and the years ahead, not even a whole day, just the next fifteen minutes or so.

One step at a time.

But what *was* she to do? Should she buy another horse? If she did, where should she go? Or should she stay? But she couldn't stay in the forest for ever . . .

She felt cold and went back into the caravan. It was a mess, paintings everywhere, on the dresser and the bunks, and charcoal drawings pinned higgledy-piggledy to the walls.

Most of her work was done in poster paint. She liked hard bright colours: vivid greens, cerulean blues, and reds that leapt out at one.

She began to gather them up. None of them were much more than eighteen inches square, for the caravan was too small for large works. She made a pile and then opened the big drawer under one of the bunks and was about to put the new series in with all the earlier paintings when she thought she ought to go through them once again, re-sort them, get them into chronological order. She had too many and this would enable her to throw away repeats or those with which she wasn't satisfied.

She paused on her knees in front of the drawer and riffled through the paintings. There were sixty or seventy of them. Every style imaginable. They represented her life, she thought. This drawer was her whole existence. In a moment of inspiration she knew what she wanted. She would sort them into sequence and they would make a pictorial diary of her life.

Then she would put each one up on the small easel and judge it just as they judged entries for the Royal Academy. She would be her own hanging committee! If a painting passed she would keep it and mount it. If it didn't, then into the fire with it!

This would take hours and hours. She could do a little at a time. Not too much. She could save it up, look forward to it.

She pulled the paintings from the drawer on to the floor. A narrative of a life. Only a few days ago she had painted herself as a child. That would have to go in the first pile: the childhood pile. Then there would be the boarding school pile. And after that the pile she thought of as her wandering time.

She picked up a piece of cartridge paper. It went into the childhood pile. Here the rabbit was very red and very big.

' "My Life", by Rachel Nihill,' she said out loud.

Macrae, Silver and Eddie Twyford stopped at a pub near Chepstow for a pint and a sandwich and went over the meeting.

'It's odd,' Silver said.

'What is?'

'She's drawn to the rough trade – like her mother.'

'But for different reasons, laddie. Robson Healey would have probably been an exciting sort of bloke for the mother. But Chris . . . She said he was *kind* to her. That's what some people want most.'

Silver looked at Macrae under his eyebrows. Was that

Macrae talking from his own experience? Once, when drunk, he had rambled on about his father's brutality both to himself and to his mother. This morning it had been oddly embarrassing to hear the great thief taker confess to loving his mother.

'Drink up,' Macrae said. 'Let's go and see this friend of her mother's . . . What's his name?'

Silver looked at his notebook and read out: 'Charles Harris, Weyford Marina, Surrey. I checked. It's near Guildford on the river Wey.'

He saw the entry below that in his notebook. It was a note to himself to check that Ronald Purvis was still serving his time in gaol. He hadn't had a chance yet. He'd do that when he got back to London.

He said, 'You ever come across the letters BOLTOP written on the back flap of an envelope, guv'nor?'

'BOLTOP? Never. Why?'

'Someone addressed an envelope like that to Zoe.'

'You heard of SWALK?' Eddie said. 'Sealed With A Loving Kiss. When I was doing my National Service lots of the blokes used to put that on their envelopes. I remember some of 'em put BOLTOP too. Better On Lips Than On Paper.'

'Not only the army,' Macrae said. 'They do it a lot in the nick.'

'Who?' Silver said.

'Prisoners. Some of them don't like to write personal messages to their wives or girlfriends knowing the censors are going to read the letters. So they put it on the envelopes. Zoe's was probably a joke. Come on, let's go and see Charles Harris Esquire.'

As they drove back along the M4, Silver comforted himself with the thought that if the envelope had come from Purvis then it meant he was still in prison and had got someone who'd served his sentence to push it through his letter-flap. But he'd check anyway.

Chapter 12

'Luncheon is served,' Ronnie said with a flourish, bringing the tray into the bedroom.

He was feeling chipper. He'd learnt that from old Crowhurst. The old sod often said he was feeling chipper. God knew why since he was in the bleedin' nick.

His mother was facing away from the door. When she turned he saw that her eyes were red.

Bloody waterworks. If it wasn't one end it was the other.

'You all right?' he asked.

' 'Course I'm not all right!'

This was an old scene.

'It's all that sherry.'

'All that *what*?'

'Alcoholic remorse. That's what it is. Makes you feel rotten and brings on the old tears.'

'That's what you think, is it?'

'It's what I know.'

He remembered old Crowhurst brewing hooch in the nick out of potato peelings and anything else he could steal from the kitchen. He used to drink a half a gallon of the stuff at a time. It's a wonder it hadn't killed him. Then the whining and the crying and the feeling sorry for himself.

She asked for a little pink bed-jacket and he settled the tray on her lap.

'What's that?' she said.

'Luncheon meat.'

'I don't want luncheon meat.'

'What d'you want then?'

'I want proper meals! It's bad enough being where I am without having to eat this muck!'

'You expecting me to cook?'

'Why not? You don't do anything else.'

'I'm not bloody cooking.'

'And watch your tongue.' She moved the luncheon meat about on the plate. 'You never give me a hot meal.'

'You get Meals-on-Wheels.'

'Ugh! They smell of those aluminium dishes they keep them warm in. Horrible.'

'You're lucky. Years ago you wouldn't have got someone bringing you in a meal.'

'Years ago children looked after their parents and cooked for them properly.'

'You got a house, a roof over your head, you got a telly, you got a car—'

'And that's another thing! Did you take my car last night?'

'Only for a while.'

'I've told you before. If you want to use the car you ask me. Where are the keys? Bring me the keys! I'll keep the keys and if you want to use it you ask.'

'Why? It's no good to you.'

'Because it's my car, that's why.'

'You're never gonna drive the bloody thing again.'

'Maybe I will, maybe I won't. It's no business of yours.'

'You won't! Face it!'

She threw her head to one side as though to reject such an idea then said, 'You got a girl? Is that why you want it? You doing things to girls in my car?'

He opened his mouth to deny it, then turned away and looked into the street.

'You have, haven't you? Answer me!'

There was a trace of panic in her voice.

He smiled to himself. 'All right, what if I have?'

'Ronald! Are you telling me the truth? *Have* you got someone?'

'Name's Barbara.'

'Barbara? Barbara who?'

'Never mind who, you wouldn't know the name anyway.'

'Don't talk to your mother like that. If you're going out with young ladies I've a right to know. What does she do anyway?'

'She's a therapist.'

'A what? What sort of therapist?'

'Counsellor.'

'That's what you need, young man. Counselling.'

'For Christ's sake, stop calling me "young man". I'm twenty-nine.'

'Therapist! What would a therapist want going round with you?'

'What all girls want.'

'Don't be filthy. You bring her round here and let me meet her. Where did you find her anyway?'

'Wimbledon Common.'

'What were you doing on Wimbledon Common? Does your parole officer know you go to Wimbledon Common?'

'It's got nothing to do with him. So long as I report in once a week that's all he's got to worry about. Anyway, I was bird-watching.'

'Liar. You wouldn't know a budgerigar from a Canada goose.'

'Yes I would. There're lots of things I know that you don't know I know.'

'You're a rotten little liar. Just like your father. Weak and rotten.'

She said it with such vehemence that she was momentarily exhausted. It was a signal. They both drew back.

'Eat your lunch,' he said. 'I'll fetch the tray later.'

'Where are you going?'

'Nowhere.'

The word, or the way he said it, seemed to get through to her, for she turned to him and said, 'Don't listen to me.

I don't really mean it. You're a good boy. Remember what you used to say to me when you were a little boy?'

He knew but stuck to the ritual. 'What?'

'I used to say to you, "Who're you going to marry when you grow up?" And you know what you used to say?'

'Yeah.'

'You used to say, "I'm going to marry you. You're my best girl." '

The expression on her face was pleading.

Bloody old cow.

'You still are,' he said. 'You're my best girl.'

He went to his bedroom, picked up a martial arts magazine and lay down. Soon his mother would call. He would fetch the tray. He would take her to the bathroom. He would make her bed . . .

'This is what the rest of your life will be,' the Prison psychiatrist had said. 'Prison. Freedom for a short time. And prison again.'

'I'm never coming back,' Ronnie had said.

'I'm glad to hear it, but it's what everyone says. You're in with Crowhurst, aren't you?'

'Yes, sir.'

'You don't want to end up like him, he's been in more than he's been out. He's what we call a "lazy paedophile". He interferes with his own family because they're around and he's too lazy to go and interfere with someone else's. You've never been in trouble before, have you?'

'No, sir.'

'Is that where the policeman hit you?'

Ronnie flinched and jerked his head back as the psychiatrist seemed about to touch his cheek.

'Yes, sir.'

'It's left quite a scar. Is that why you've grown your hair? To hide it?'

'Yes, sir.'

'And that's why they call you Veronica Lake? Because of the hair?'

'Yes, sir.'

'Do you mind being called that?'

'No, sir. Not if it makes them happy.'

The psychiatrist looked at Ronnie closely, shifted a number of papers on his desk, picked one up, put it down, glanced at another.

'We're going to give you a chance, Purvis. An experiment's been set up at a prison in Hampshire. Have you heard of Granton?'

'No, sir.'

'It's one of the new prisons. There's a therapy unit. A self-help unit for people like you and some of the other Rule 43 prisoners. I'm not saying it'll be easy. Some of the group sessions are pretty tough. The other inmates will make you face up to things you don't want to face up to. Things you've forgotten or hidden away inside yourself. You understand what I'm saying?'

'Yes, sir.'

'At least it'll give you a chance.' He sat back. 'More than six thousand sexual offenders are convicted every year in Britain, Purvis, and we can treat less than seven per cent of them. Most choose as you've done to be segregated from the others under Rule 43.

'I'm not saying I blame you. Up to now the theory's been that ordinary prisoners will assault sex offenders, make your lives hell. At Granton there are no Rule 43 prisoners; no "nonces" no "wrong 'uns". You'll all be together; sex offenders, murderers, robbers. So far not a single sex offender has been attacked. But there's always a first time. It's up to you, Purvis. You'll have to make a decision.'

At first Granton had been tough, but at least he wasn't a paedophile. In the hierarchy of sexual offenders he was a would-be rapist with a knife. It gave him a kind of standing among the wet-mouthed nonces who'd interfered with defenceless little girls and boys.

He learned to play the system. The name of the game was sincerity. So when they'd questioned him about his background he'd been explicit. He'd told them of his father who had died when he was a teenager, but not what his mother thought of him or how she had acted towards him.

He told them about watching his mother in the bath. That had made a deep impression. It was something most of them had done yet no one had mentioned it until he did.

He told them of the day he'd had a bitter row with his mother and gone out by himself and had wandered about north London and had fetched up in a deserted garden and a young woman had come jogging by . . .

After a few months he became a leader in discussion groups. He spoke about good and evil and drew an analogy between the white and the black knights.

The woman psychiatrist had been particularly interested in that. And when she asked him how he saw himself he said he was a mixture of the two. And one of the other prisoners had said, 'Aren't we all?'

She had nodded and smiled to herself and written something down. 'Can you define normality?'

The group had thought for a long time. Ronnie had read something in a novel about the subject and said, 'I don't think there is a state of normality. None of us is absolutely normal. It's just that some people make better adjustments than others.'

'That's good, Ronnie,' she'd said. 'That's very good.'

Another time, in what they called 'one-to-one', she'd said to him, 'What do you think of yourself, Ronnie?'

'I'm devious, snidey. I'm a nasty person.'

'Don't you think that's an adjustment too?'

'What, Doctor?'

'Just being able to say that.'

Then there was a visit from an Oxford University criminologist who had helped to set up the experiment and he'd had a long interview with Ronnie and then he'd said to him,

'*Part of the experiment is placing you back in society. Do you think you're ready for that?*'

'*Yes, sir. I'm not coming back, sir.*'

The criminologist looked at Ronnie's papers. 'They all say that, but I think you might be one of the exceptions . . .'

In her caravan deep in the Forest of Dean, Rachel Nihill had stopped sorting her paintings. She was tense and uneasy. She had thought that the process of sorting might help her. She had not expected the opposite reaction. It had come when she had found the very first painting in the rabbit series. It had been done at school and then hidden away. The shock of seeing it again was like a physical blow. The rabbit was huge, red, and menacing. She couldn't look at it. It seemed, in its aggressive way, to want to come off the canvas and attack her.

She found a kitchen knife. She drove it into the rabbit, slashing and slashing until the canvas was ripped to pieces. Then she collected the pieces and took them to the old mine workings and threw them on the rubbish pile which she and Chris had started.

Chapter 13

The river Wey, which flows through Surrey, isn't much more than thirty miles long from start to finish, and what is rather grandly called the Wey Navigation is only about half that distance.

Eddie Twyford, after the third argument that day with Macrae, found Weyford Marina in mid-afternoon. It was tucked away in a basin off the main river and surrounded by trees. A sign at the gate said, 'Narrow Boats for Hire'.

Macrae and Silver walked along the edge of the basin. It was packed with boats, each around forty feet long but only six feet wide. They were of a type that had been specially designed for Britain's narrow canals as far back as the nineteenth century. They were moored tightly against each other in rows and reminded Silver of sardines in a can. A large wooden hut, on which was painted: 'OFFICE. S. STAPLETON. PROP.', stood at the far end where a bantam of a man was washing the deck of one of the boats.

'You the boss?' Macrae said.

The man was in his fifties, bald, with a sunburnt skull that shone in the sunlight.

'You looking for a boat, sir? Take your pick. This here's a Windrush Class IV. Sleeps six. Lister diesel. Take you anywhere. Absolute comfort and safety. You're going to tell me that you've never been in a narrow boat before and I'm going to tell you, sir, that driving one of these is as easy as pushing a pram. Half an hour's instruction is all you need, sir. You thinking of it for yourself and the family? Couldn't make a better choice. All centrally heated. I been in this business thirty-one years and never had a dud boat.' He banged the hull. 'British steel. You won't find better—'

Macrae held up his hand. 'I asked if you were the boss.'

'Sole proprietor. Sammy Stapleton. Yes, sir, best time of the year. Too early in the season for the crowds. River's clear. No queueing at the locks.'

Macrae held up his warrant card. The man squinted at it and said, 'Oh Christ!' He put down the long-handled mop and wiped his forehead with his handkerchief. 'It's about time.' His tone was aggrieved. 'I phoned yesterday.'

'What about?' Silver said.

'What about? About the break-in, of course. What else? They smashed the windows on two of the boats this time. Took mattresses, blankets, a whole list of stuff.'

'We're not the Surrey police,' Macrae said. 'We're from London. Is there a Charles Harris here?'

'Charlie?'

Macrae stared at him. 'If that's what you call him?'

'What's he done then?'

Macrae said, 'Please don't make me repeat everything.'

'We want to ask him a few questions,' Silver said.

'He ain't done nothin' wrong then?'

'Not that we know of.'

'He's at Benstead Lock. Or should be by now. Testin' his engines. He's *always* testin' his engines.'

'He works here?'

'You could say that. Some would say that. I know I pay him to work here.'

Sammy Stapleton began to wash the deck vigorously. 'This is what he should be at. We got the season starting next week. All these boats to clean out. Christ . . . I dunno . . . '

'Where's Benstead Lock?' Macrae asked. He was beginning to lose patience.

'See the railway line?' Stapleton pointed to a viaduct about two miles downstream. 'Lock's just this side of it.'

'How do we get there?' Macrae said. 'Is there a road?'

92

'This is a river, mate. If it was a road we'd be hiring out cars.'

The two detectives went back to the car.

'See if you can find a way along the bank,' Macrae said to Eddie Twyford.

'Along there?' Eddie's voice was shrill with indignation. 'You got to be joking, guv'nor.'

'For Christ's sake, Eddie, just *do* it!'

Keeping one wheel on the towpath and the other on the grass bank, Eddie gingerly took the Ford along the water's edge. Silver hung on to the grab-handle above the rear seat. Macrae sat upright hanging on to nothing, pretending the violent bumps weren't happening.

They came to Benstead Lock.

They were only about thirty-five miles from London yet they might have been in the wilds of Devon. They were surrounded by lush water meadows where a few surprised cows paused in their feeding to watch them. In the distance a train pulled out of Weyford station, but it seemed to belong to another world. A narrow boat was moored a few yards downstream of Benstead Lock from which emerged the sounds of loud rock music. Macrae's granitic expression changed to one of distaste.

The boat was smaller than the ones at the boatyard but very smart in its dark-blue and gold livery. All the fittings were of highly polished brass. Painted on the bows were the words PASSION PALACE.

'Anyone at home?' Macrae called. They stepped aboard. The radio was on deck and Macrae switched it off. The silence was startling.

'What the hell's going on?' a voice shouted from the engine compartment.

'Charles Harris?' Macrae called.

'Who wants him?'

They let themselves down into the saloon. It occupied the entire forward area of the boat. There were two easy chairs, a television set and a large unmade double bed. Silver saw a couple of empty champagne bottles on a low table and an ashtray filled with butts.

'What the hell do you want?' a voice said behind them.

They turned and Silver saw a man of about thirty, big and powerful, with curly hair and blue eyes. His shirt was unbuttoned to the navel and his jeans, like his hands, were covered in grease. He exuded a kind of animal vigour, a maleness that Silver would have liked to possess himself.

'I asked you what you wanted.' Harris said.

Macrae said, 'I get bloody tired of people always asking what I want. Are you Charles Harris?'

'You deaf or something?'

'Please,' Macrae said. 'I've had a hard day.' He examined the nearest chair for dirt or foreign objects and then sat down. 'Tell him who we are, laddie.'

Silver told him.

'So?' Harris said.

'So are you Charles Harris?' Macrae said.

'Yes. Is this about the break-in?'

'No, it isn't about the break-in.'

Harris's eyes shifted quickly around the saloon, seeing what they were seeing.

'Well, what d'you want with me then?'

'We'll get to that.'

'Is this your boat?' Silver said.

Harris nodded.

'Why d'you call it the *Passion Palace*? The others up there are called *Windrush* or *Willow* . . . names like that.'

'It's just a joke.'

'Doesn't seem to go with the boat.'

'Yeah . . . well . . . '

'Do you know Mrs Robson Healey?' Macrae asked.

'I . . . yeah . . . I know her. She's got a cottage. That one over there.'

He pointed to a small white-washed cottage crouched against the side of a low hill about half a mile from the river.

94

'Haven't a clue.'

'Was she the one who gave you the champagne?'

'That's right, chief.'

'You have lots of women aboard? Is that why it's called the *Passion Palace*?'

'That's right, chief.'

Macrae rose slowly. 'All right, Harris. That'll do for now.' A look of relief crossed the man's face. 'You don't mind if I have one of these, do you? Remind me of what to buy.' He lifted one of the champagne bottles by putting his fingers in the neck.

'Don't go away without letting the local police know where you are.'

'Why? I'm telling you I haven't done a thing.'

'And *I'm* telling *you*,' Macrae said.

They went back to the car.

Silver said, 'He's got three wrenches in the engine compartment the same make as the one we found at Healey's house.'

'Good lad. Keep an eye on the boat. As soon as you lose sight of it tell me. And Eddie, you stop the car.'

Silver watched out of the back window as Eddie slowly ground along the towpath. A bend in the river and a stand of trees blocked out his view of the boat and he told Eddie. The car stopped.

Macrae said, 'I want to see what our friend does.'

Silver followed him to a patch of scrub willow from which they could see the boat. They hadn't been watching for more than a couple of minutes when Harris left the boat and began to walk towards Mrs Healey's cottage.

He reached the front door, looked carefully around, and opened it with a key he had taken from his pocket.

'I thought so,' Macrae said.

Keeping to what cover there was, the two reached the cottage. The windows were heavily barred. Standing close to the walls they could look into the ground-floor rooms.

'Does she like boating?' Macrae said.

'Not that I know of.'

'How do you know her then?'

'I met her one day. She was walking along the towpath. I was working on the boat. We chatted. Listen, this is about the murder, isn't it? I mean I read all about it in the press. It was on the television.'

'That's right,' Macrae said.

'But that's got nothing to do with me, for Christ's sake! I mean I never even knew him. What're you writing down?'

' "I never even knew him," ' Silver read from his notes and smiled at Harris.

'Oh.'

Macrae leaned back in the chair and closed his eyes. The air was warm and he'd been up since five-thirty. He was feeling sleepy and had an overwhelming desire to climb on to the double bed. He said, 'She says she was at her cottage last weekend, and that you can corroborate it.'

'That's right. She was down.'

'How d'you know?' Silver said.

'She came and asked if I'd do something for her in the cottage. I'd helped her once or twice before.'

'What had happened?'

'Couldn't get the electrics to work. Main fuse box kept on tripping. I found a faulty plug and fixed it.'

Macrae said, 'She's a good-looking woman.'

'Yeah. Bit long in the tooth for me.'

'You like them young, do you?'

'Hey! Don't get me wrong. I'm not into kids. Nothing like that.'

'When was this?'

'Saturday evening, I think.'

'You think?'

'Yeah . . . Saturday evening.'

'What about Sunday evening?'

'No, it was Saturday evening.'

'Where were you on Sunday evening?'

'Sunday . . . let's see . . . '

Macrae said, 'You're not a partner, are you? Nothing like that?'

'You mean with Sammy?'

'That's right.'

'No. I look after the boats. Engines mainly. I'm good with my hands.'

'You mind if I look round?' Silver said. 'While you talk to Mr Macrae.'

Silver turned and ducked through the doorway.

'Hang on, I didn't say—'

Macrae said, 'So if she was here on Sunday evening you couldn't have known? Is that right?'

He looked over his shoulder 'Listen he's got no bloody—'

'Is that right!'

'Yeah . . . yeah . . . '

'Don't worry about my partner. He won't break anything.'

'I don't like people—'

'Let's go back to Sunday. The day Robson Healey was killed. You say she wasn't here on Sunday?'

'No, I didn't say that.'

'I thought you did.'

'You're mixing me up.' Again he swung his head round to look for Silver.

'I wouldn't want to do that,' Macrae said. 'Take your time. Get it straight.'

Macrae picked up one of the empty champagne bottles, looked at it carefully. 'Bollinger '78,' he said. 'Good stuff. I'm thinking of having a little celebration myself. What's a bottle like this cost?'

'I dunno.'

'Vintage always costs more. I usually buy non-vintage myself. Can't afford stuff like this on a copper's salary. Must be thirty or forty quid.'

'It was a present.'

'Both bottles?'

'Yeah.'

'Who from?'

'Grateful customer.'

Silver came back into the saloon. 'Very nice,' h

'We were talking about champagne,' Macrae sa much would you say that was worth?'

Silver looked at the label. 'I'm no expert, guv'nor got to be thirty pounds a bottle.'

'That's what I thought.'

He turned to Harris. 'So you've done work for Mrs in the past?'

'Yeah.'

'But not on Sunday afternoon or evening?'

'No.'

'You just fixed her electric plug on Saturday and you di see her again.'

'Yeah.'

'Where were you anyway on Sunday evening?' Sil asked.

'I . . . on the boat . . . yeah . . . on the boat . . . '

'Where?'

'Downstream. Near Send.'

'By yourself?'

'No.'

'Well, who were you with?'

'You know how it is, chief . . . '

'No, I don't know.'

'Well, I had this girl on bo—'

'Girl? How old?'

'No! No! Christ, I told you. I call her girl but she's nineteen . . . twenty.'

'What's her name?' Silver said.

There was a fractional pause and then he said, 'Pamela. Yeah. Pamela.'

'You don't sound too sure.'

'It's just that I don't know her last name.'

'Or where she lives?'

Everything was expensive, from the luxury kitchen to the grey and white living room with its smoked glass coffee table, white tufted carpet, and black leather sofas.

Charles Harris was emptying ashtrays and dropping bottles into a large plastic refuse bag. He wiped the ashtrays, then the surface of the table. He was looking round to see if he had missed anything when Macrae opened the front door and walked in.

'More champagne?' Macrae said. 'Another gift from someone who's last name you can't remember and whose address you don't know?'

He took the refuse bag from Harris and fished out a bottle and said, 'Bollinger '78. You're a lucky man, Harris. And what's this?' He pulled out a bottle of Russian vodka and turned to Silver. 'This is the real stuff, laddie. Khrushchev used to get pissed on this.' He shook the bag and several other bottles clinked together. 'It must have been quite a party. Sit down, Harris.'

Harris sat on one of the leather sofas, the two detectives sat opposite him. Macrae lit a thin panatella and leaned back. 'You've been a naughty boy, Harris. You've not been telling the truth. Now let's go back to the beginning.'

Harris looked down at his big hands. Oil and grease were permanently imbedded in the quicks of his fingernails.

'What do you want to know?'

'How did you meet her?'

'Through his partner.'

'Whose partner?'

'Robson Healey's.'

'What's his name?'

'Howard Rollins. He used to hire one of the boats. She used to meet him here.'

'Go on . . . '

They talked until the light began to fade. By this time Harris had lost much of his self-confidence, and when Macrae reminded him, as they left, not to go anywhere without leaving his address with the local police, he nodded quietly and said, 'Okay, chief.'

Night came to the forest.

Rachel had always been afraid of the dark.

Night . . . the dark . . . death . . . decay . . .

Even the words frightened her and usually she loved words.

She lay in the caravan with the hissing gas-light hanging from the roof. She had been lying like this for hours, trying to make up her mind what to do. She was no nearer a decision. She wanted to leave. She wanted to stay.

As dusk had entered the forest she had thought she had seen a man walking towards her. But then, when she looked again, he had vanished.

It might have been a trick of the light. The movement of a branch.

But there *were* people who lived in the forest. She was sure of that. She had heard them singing.

This was an old forest, part of the Great Forest that had once covered England in Saxon times. Then it would have been filled with lepers and gangrels, witches and spirits, thieves and robbers and murderers. Over the centuries trees had been felled for building houses and ships and making charcoal. The forest was not what it had been but the old magic was there still.

Was that singing she heard now?

She felt a tightening of her chest as she listened.

Bye baby bunting . . . Daddy's gone a-hunting . . . Gone to get a rabbit skin . . . To wrap the baby bunting in . . .

Her nanny had sung it to her as a child. Even then it had made her uneasy. She remembered that.

Now, of course, it wasn't the rabbit *skin* that worried her. It was the rabbit itself. The red rabbit . . .

She sat up and tried to clear her chest.

She listened. But all she could hear was the hissing of the gas.

Chapter 14

Leo Silver was never quite sure why Macrae used the Goodwood Sporting Club. His sister Ruth said it was because police and criminals shared the same desires and the same world. If she was right then it fitted, for the club, in spite of its grand name, was used solely by London villains.

It was where they came to relax, to play kalooki, to show off their 'wedges' – the tightly packed wads of ten and twenty-pound notes kept together by silver clips – to smoke their expensive Havanas, to flaunt their solid gold bracelets and rings, and their mohair suits and vicuña coats, their Gucci watches. It was a mutual admiration society housed in a building between The Strand and the river.

No one had ever asked Macrae to join. Silver wasn't even sure there was a membership system apart from the general membership of the criminal fraternity. Macrae simply used the place and Silver had never seen anyone object.

The crowded room, with its choking layers of cigar smoke, the sporting prints on the wall, and the statue of the jockey at the door, reminded Silver of a scene from an old movie. He watched Macrae shoulder his way to the bar.

Those at the top of the tree, the strong men from the East End, the inheritors of the Krays and Richardsons, who liked to trace their criminal lineage as far back as Jack Spot himself, watched Macrae with open hostility. But the lesser villains, the con artists and the pickpockets, greeted him deferentially.

Was this why he came, Silver wondered? The need for reassurance? Or was it all part of Macrae's special relationship with the Metropolitan Police?

Silver knew the lonely life he led in Battersea, he knew about the tarts who came in as surrogate wives, the drinking bouts that lasted a full weekend. As Silver had tried to get him to bed after one such binge, Macrae had talked of his background and Silver had sensed he was terrified of ending up an alcoholic like his father.

The police force was his family and his crutch. It was possible that to Macrae the Goodwood was just an extension of the police; the dark side, the underbelly. It was a fact of life that he was happier in the company of either fellow officers or criminals than members of the general public.

They had come back late in the afternoon from Surrey and had gone into Cannon Row police station. Macrae had read all the messages from the incident room, the most important of which was a brief report confirming that the wrench was the weapon that had killed Robson Healey. But there were no prints on it nor had it ever been used for its original purpose.

There was also a message saying that Lysander Goater had been located and they were bringing him in.

'Who's Lysander Goater, guv'nor?' Silver had asked Macrae.

'Rambo put me on to him. He runs a string of high-class girls in the Chelsea area.'

Then Silver had asked the desk sergeant to check on the whereabouts of Ronald Arthur Purvis and they had come on to the Goodwood.

Silver watched the big man pick up the drinks and come across the room.

'Pint for you . . . pint for me . . . dram for you . . . dram for me . . .' He raised the shot glass of whisky to Silver.

'Slàinte.'

'Cheers.'

They drank.

Macrae swallowed a third of his pint and then sat back, lit a slim panatella and said, 'What d'you think of Harris, laddie?'

'He's a liar and a fornicator,' Silver said. 'But then we all are from time to time and you can't charge a man with that.'

'Yes, but was he lying the second time round?'

The three men had eyed each other, Silver and Macrae on one cream leather sofa, Harris on the other.

'Tell me about this Howard Collins,' Macrae had said.

'I only know what I heard and saw. I didn't know at the time who he was. She told me later.'

'How did you meet him?'

'Like any other punter who comes to hire a boat. I mean we get quite a bit of the dirty weekend trade. It's not all families and kids. When you think about it, what could be safer? You're miles from anywhere, no one in sight.'

'Every weekend?'

'Only the weekends her husband was away. He was doing it somewhere else, see? Had his own plane. He'd hop over to France for a weekend. Take his own party, his own floozies. Have a ball. And she was left alone. Not surprising she wanted some fun for herself.'

'You say he was Healey's partner?'

'Yeah, not now, but back in the early days. I didn't inquire. You don't. Then after a few months he got tired of driving boats through locks and along canals just for a bit of the old humpy-bumpy. So he bought this cottage.'

'She used to come here?' Macrae said.

'Yeah. She'd come to the marina and leave her car there and I'd drive her along the towpath the way you came. There's a back lane to the cottage but she didn't like to take it. But even so her husband found out. I mean if you've private detectives watching you it doesn't really matter where you leave your car. She didn't think about that, see. She thought he was having his own good time and he wasn't really bothered with her any longer. But blokes like Healey . . . when they get married . . . the wife becomes a possession like a car or a boat. Anyway, Healey sent down a couple of blokes to have a chat with Collins. Warn him off, like. I was down on the boat testing my engines when she comes running down screaming that they're killing him. By the time I get there they're gone.'

'You didn't hurry,' Macrae said.

'I'm not looking for a medal. Anyway, Collins is lying on the floor, blood all over his face.'

'Is that why you're so scared?' Silver asked.

Harris's head came up sharply. 'Scared?'

'You're frightened.'

He wiped a hand over his face. 'Well it's . . . it's unsettling. And Healey isn't the sort of bloke you mess around with.'

'He's dead,' Macrae said. 'He can't hurt you now. How did you and she—?'

'Well, Collins wasn't having any more after that. When he recovered he took off for Spain. Healey bought him out. He still had the cottage though. She rented it from him. Only bought it later, after she and Healey had split up.'

'You took Collins's place, then?'

'You could say that.'

'Does he still live in Spain?'

'I dunno. He had a place in London as well. Bayswater, I think.'

'Tell us about Sunday night,' Macrae said. 'You were here, weren't you?'

'Yeah. Saturday night on the boat. Sunday night here.'

'She likes partying, then?' Silver said.

'Does she ever!'

'You see her in London?'

'Never. Only here at weekends. She always telephones, tells me what to buy. I mean food- and drink-wise.'

'You're a sort of caretaker, then?' Silver said. 'Does she pay you? I mean a wage.'

'Listen, I'm not her bloody fancy-man if that's what you think. I don't get paid by the inch. I get paid for looking after this place.'

'Did you get drunk on Sunday?' Macrae said.

'Yeah. We had a party at lunchtime. Can't remember a bloody thing after that. Not until I woke up about ten that night.'

'Was she here?'

'I dunno. I woke up on this sofa. She may have been in the upstairs bedroom. All I wanted was my own bed so I went down to the boat.'

'What about her car?'

'I can't remember seeing *any*thing.'

Soon after that they left.

Macrae finished his drink and said to Silver, 'You know something, laddie? I think he thinks she might have done her husband in.'

'Why would she do that?'

'For her freedom. Maybe he said he'd never give her her freedom without a fight. Maybe she didn't want to fight. I don't know, but it's possible. I mean you heard what Harris said about Healey and possessions. He could be right there. And if Harris was drunk enough she could have gone up to London, killed Healey and been back before he knew she'd gone. That's the way his mind's working. That's why he was cleaning up the place. That's why he told us he was drunk between lunchtime and ten o'clock. That's why he said he wasn't sure if she was in the house. He's giving himself escape routes. Anyway, we've got to go and have another little talk with Mrs Robson Healey.'

'Mr Macrae.'

Macrae and Silver glanced up. A big man in his forties, with a wide expressionless face and hard eyes, was standing at their table.

'What d'you want, Stoker?' Macrae said.

'A word with you.'

'Can't you see I'm busy?'

Stoker made no move.

'Oh, Christ . . . '

Macrae rose. Silver remained seated.

'What?' Macrae asked.

'Mr Gorman wants to see you.'

Macrae's face darkened. 'What the hell's that got to do with you, Stoker? You his messenger-boy now?'

Stoker's face remained expressionless. 'That's out of order, Mr Macrae.'

'Oh fuck off, there's a good lad.'

Stoker nodded slowly. 'You've been told, Mr Macrae.'

He walked away.

Silver was watching the other villains. Their heads had come up at the start of the conversation and their eyes had rested on Macrae. Their expressions were cold. It was a coldness that caused Silver's flesh to creep.

'You seen Scales, George?' Detective Chief Superintendent Wilson came into Macrae's office.

'Why? Does he want to see me?'

'He's doing his nut. He says you took a driver after he told you not to.'

'Well?'

Macrae had had just enough to drink feel the old belligerency begin to surface.

'Oh Jesus, George, you just won't be told, will you?'

'I haven't got time for pricks like Scales.'

'Have you been drinking?'

'Listen, Les—'

'You listen. I don't give a fuck, but Scales is paranoid. I told you that. He's been buggering around all day trying to find out how much coffee we use, how much tea, how much toilet paper. Then he finds you've got Twyford. I thought he was going through the bloody roof. It's going to be hard enough having him around without you making things worse.'

The desk sergeant put his head round the door. 'There's a Lysander Goater in interview room three, Mr Macrae.'

'A *what?*' Wilson said.

'Rambo put me on to him.' He turned. 'Go home, Les. Have a good night's sleep and give Beryl a kiss for me. And stop worrying about me. It's my arse.'

Silver was already in interview room three. 'This is Lysander Goater, guv'nor,' he said as Macrae entered. The big man only grunted. It was as much a grunt of surprise as a greeting.

The surprise was at the sight of the small, neatly dressed black man who sat at the table, his hands demurely on his lap. His face was thin, and his eyes framed by large black spectacles. He was wearing a dark suit and a clerical collar.

'Lysander, eh?' Macrae said. 'Where did you get a name like that?'

The young man said, 'I must protest. Your people took me out of a prayer meeting. For no reason at all.'

'Well, like the man said, we can always find a reason.'

'But what am I supposed to have done, Inspector?'

'Detective Superintendent.'

'My apologies.' The voice was educated. 'But you still haven't answered my question. And I would like to see my solicitor.'

'Why, have you done something wrong?'

'You seem to think so.'

'Not at all, laddie. I've got a few questions, that's all. Answer them and you're back in your prayer meeting in half an hour. We'll even take you back by car.'

The young man relaxed.

Macrae said, 'That's better. Now tell me about "Lysander", Lysander.'

'My father was in the Grenadier Guards.'

Macrae raised his eyebrows in disbelief.

'Oh, not in the regiment. They didn't take blacks then. No, he worked in the canteen as a dishwasher. He named me Lysander.'

107

Macrae turned to Silver. 'It's like Round Britain Quiz, isn't it? Give me a clue, Lysander.'

Goater smiled slightly. 'You're the detective, Mr Macrae.'

'Right, let's see then. Grenadier Guards. Army. What does an army do? It goes to battle. Marches into battle. Marching song. What's the marching song of the Grenadier Guards, laddie?'

'I don't know, guv'nor?'

'They didn't teach you that at the university, then?'

'No.'

'Hot or cold, Lysander?'

'Very warm.'

Macrae began tapping out a marching rhythm on the table and said, '"Some talk of Alexander/And some of Hercules./Of Hector and Lysander/And such great men as these . . . " That's the verse, isn't it, Lysander?'

'That's the verse, Mr Macrae. But you didn't take me out of a prayer meeting to discuss army marching songs.'

'That's right, Lysander. It's to discuss girls.'

'Girls?' Goater smiled again. 'I thought so. It's a case of mistaken identity.'

Having solved the knotty question of Lysander's baptism, Macrae was in a sunny mood. 'Now, now, Lysander, let's not spoil things.' He took a sheet of paper from his pocket and unfolded it. He began to read. '"Lysander Goater, twenty-nine, no fixed address . . . " Well, do you want me to read them all? . . . Breaking and entering . . . armed robbery . . . uttering threats and menaces . . . extortion . . . Goodness me, Lysander, you're raising the London crime statistics single-handed. Now tell me, how many Lysander Goaters d'you think are in the London telephone directory?'

Goater looked at Silver, gave him a wide smile as though to apologise, then turned back to Macrae. 'How can I help you?'

Chapter 15

'Stop!' Linda Macrae said. 'It says all the files will be destroyed.'

'Why?' David Leitman asked.

'God knows. Let me look in the instruction book.'

They were staring at the warning notice on the screen of his new word processor. He had bought it the previous day and had spent most of the intervening hours trying to make sense of the soft-ware instructions.

'All I want to do is get something on disc and get it to stay there.' His voice was tightly controlled. 'Now this damned machine tells me I'm going to destroy all the files on the disc. But there aren't any files on the disc! That's the whole point! That's what I'm trying to do. Get files on the bloody thing!'

She burst out laughing.

He said, 'I think they should take the people who wrote this book of instructions and make them go to school again and learn how to write English and not this terrible computerspeak!'

'Why don't we give it a break, David?'

They were in his study, hypnotised by the green screen. They had spent the previous evening there as well, and a strange computer-induced intimacy had arisen between them, at least it seemed so to Linda.

She had the feeling they were the only two people left in the world as they fiddled unsuccessfully with the various functions of word processing. So far they had managed to get, 'Now is the time for all good men to come to the aid of the party,' on to the screen but had not been able to save it on disc.

Hours had vanished. The previous night it had been nearly one o'clock before she had got to bed and yet the time had sped so fast she had thought it was not much more than ten.

'As I understood it,' he said, 'and I'm saying this with a smile and as sweetly as I know how . . . but as I understood it, you took a course in word processing.'

'I know . . . I know . . . And I feel terrible about you buying it. I thought I'd be able to figure it out in a few minutes. But I never . . . never . . . worked on anything like this!' She tapped the two-hundred-page book of instructions.

'You know what I feel like doing?'

'Hitting me!'

'God forfend!' He took her hand, squeezed it and put it down. 'I feel like throwing everything out into the street; screen, keyboard, printer, instruction book – the lot. I can always go back to using a fountain pen.'

'David, we'll work it out. You'll see.'

'I hope so.'

'Why don't you come down and have coffee and forget about it for tonight?'

'That's the best offer I've had all day.'

He switched off the word processor. 'My head feels as though it's going to split open.'

'Mine too.'

They went down to her flat and she made coffee. From the kitchen she could see into the sitting room. He was sitting on the sofa looking at the paper. It seemed so natural that she felt a catch in her throat. This is what she had been missing all these years. Just seeing a man she liked sitting on her sofa, reading the paper. It wasn't the great sexual moments, she thought – she'd never experienced one anyway – but the small domestic things, the myriad of tiny ordinary things that made up the fabric of life.

'Black?'

'With one sugar,' he said.

She put down the cup on the low table. 'Brandy?'

'If you're having one.'

'Well, I don't usually but I think I will tonight.'

'Would you mind if I smoked?'

'Of course not. I didn't know you did.'

'I gave it up about five years ago. Now I just have a cigar sometimes.' He lit a thin cheroot.

'George smoked those all the time. I love the smell.' She curled up in an armchair. 'I haven't smelled one for a long time. Not until the other night when George—'

There was an uneasy moment, then he said, 'I suppose one shouldn't but I get so damned tired of giving things up. They, the great "they", tell us all the things that are bad for us, but they never tell us what they *want* us to die of. Boredom, probably.'

They chatted comfortably about ordinary things. She told him about her daughter Susan and her present trip.

When she finished he said, 'Tell me about George.'

'George? Why?'

'Well, he's part of your life and I'm interested in peoples' lives.'

'I'm afraid mine's pretty dull if you're thinking of putting it in a book.'

He smiled at her and said, 'I'm not totally mercenary. I can be interested in people without wanting to turn them into copy.'

She inclined her head. 'I'm sorry. I didn't really mean it to sound like that. George and I go back a long way. We were at school together. He was a bit of a bruiser, a boxer. I don't think I took much notice of him then. Anyway, he was a few years above me. It was only after school that we started going out. I was looking after my father. He was dying, and George used to come home with me and he'd sit and talk to Dad for hours. I was very grateful for that. That's when he got interested in the police. Dad had been a sergeant in the uniformed branch.'

111

'When were you married?'

'Soon after Dad died. George always said I was looking for a surrogate father. Either that or someone to look after. My mother died when I was a teenager and I looked after my younger brothers and then Dad when he got ill.'

'And did you look after George?'

'I tried to. He's not the sort of person you can "look after" in that sort of way. I mean he's very independent. Doesn't like relying on anyone. Anyway, we had Susan and I was very happy, the happiest I'd been I think. But the domesticity got him down. He's not a homebody, if you know what I mean, and I suppose I am. I love being at home. But men are different.'

'I don't know that men are so different. I'm a homebody too. I had enough travelling when I was a journalist to last me a lifetime.'

'George was restless. I knew that but there wasn't anything I could do about it. We didn't have much money. So home was quite dull, I think. And his work life was pretty exciting. The Murder Squad and the Flying Squad. That sort of thing. Then he met this other person, a woman PC. They started having an affair . . . and . . . well, that's how it broke up. The marriage, I mean. I'm not sure George meant it to break up. I don't think he thought about it. George sometimes tends to act before he thinks.'

'We all do, I suppose.'

'Please don't think I'm feeling sorry for myself.'

'Of course not.'

'Because I'm not. He did me a favour in many ways. He made me think out my life. I couldn't do anything, you see. I wasn't trained. And I knew, when he left me, that I'd have to sink or swim on my own. So I took shorthand and typing and bookkeeping and word processing . . . ' She laughed. 'Maybe I shouldn't have mentioned that! And I started reading books, real books. George had started me off. He loves Dickens. You wouldn't think so but he's quite well read. So I read Dickens and Trollope and Jane

Austen. And modern writers too, of course. It was a bit like school homework at first. I mean artificial in a way. Then suddenly I started enjoying them. I mean *Great Expectations* is. well . . . '

'Great?'

'Go on, you're laughing at me.'

'Don't be absurd. How do you think anyone starts reading good stuff? That's how I started. That's how most people start. You hear about it . . . want to try . . . it's difficult at first . . . you keep with it and then as you say, suddenly – bingo. You can't stop. I've read *Great Expectations* two or three times. But I don't now, except on holiday.'

'Why not?'

'Dickens is too influential. You find yourself writing like him. And using strange names, like Magwitch or Chuzzlewit, and making characters larger than life. He could do it, I can't.'

They were silent for a moment and then he said, 'Some people don't know when they're well off.'

'How do you mean?'

'I mean George and you. He must have been out of his mind to break it up.'

'Thank you. What a very nice thing to say.'

'I'm not just saying it. I mean it.'

She studied him over the rim of her brandy glass.

'He once said to me . . . '

'What?'

'I'll tell you when I know you better.'

They looked at each other for a moment and then he rose. 'I want to stay but I won't. You've got to work tomorrow, so have I. Perhaps you'd let me take you to dinner tomorrow night.'

She hesitated, remembering what she had told herself about relationships within the same building.

He seemed to read her mind. 'See how you feel. Give me a ring tomorrow some time. I'm in all day.'

After he left she took the cups and glasses and washed

them and put them away. She was regretting he had gone. He could have stayed for another drink. But what then? Between two adults who liked and were attracted to each other there was only one logical ending.

But did she want to go to bed with him?

She had a good, uncomplicated life. Well . . . perhaps not good, but fair. Going to bed with David would change things. For her anyway, because she had never been able to have it off on a one-night stand basis. Too prudish? Or did she just want too much?

It might make her life better, transform it, but you could never be certain and she *had* to be certain, because if she fell in love and got it wrong again she would be devastated.

In their flat in Pimlico Leo and Zoe were in bed. He had told her about Rachel Nihill and her caravan and the name she had devised for it.

'How do you spell it?' Zoe said.

Leo reached for his notebook and wrote: EREWHON.

Zoe looked at it, mystified.

'What's it mean?'

'God knows. I'll look it—'

Suddenly she said, 'BOLTOP! Did you find out what it meant? Did you find out about him?'

Silver's mind went into overdrive. 'I don't know about BOLTOP,' he lied, 'but as far as he's concerned you don't have to worry. He's still inside.'

'Thank God.'

He felt her relax.

'But—'

'But what?'

'One day he'll come out, Leo. What then?'

'That's what you keep me around for, isn't it?'

It was said lightly but he wondered if she would pick it up. She didn't. Instead she put her arms around him. 'Leo . . . Leopold . . . Leopold Silver . . . Give me a kiss . . .'

* * *

In his small house in Battersea, Macrae was sitting in front of the television. The picture flickered in the dark room but the sound was turned down. On a low table was a whisky bottle and the glass. One more, he thought, and then bed.

But would one more be enough?

He remembered his father.

As a boy George would often sit in the Land-Rover outside the Highland pub when his father was drinking – no kids were allowed in the bar. He often waited in winter when there was snow or frost on the ground. Occasionally his father would come out with a packet of crisps and give them to him.

'Just one more dram, George, then we're away hame.'

Just one more . . .

Macrae poured himself one more. Then he picked up the phone and dialled Frenchy. But it rang and rang and no one answered.

Chapter 16

Rachel was chopping wood with a small hand-axe. She had collected branches earlier that morning, sawed the bigger ones into pieces and now she was splitting them. She did this deftly but slowly so as not to start her chest.

On the long slow journey to the West Country, Chris had taught her how to do this and how to saw and how to use many of his tools – she hadn't worried about her chest then. And she had learned a lot by watching him work. He was a good carpenter. And he was always worrying about his tools, sharpening the chisels on an oil stone, cleaning the rasps, and the planes and the spokeshaves. You'd have thought the tools were diamonds.

'Never hit wood with metal.'

She could still hear his voice saying it as he showed her the wooden mallet.

'Always use wood on wood.'

She could see his face in her mind. Thin, with long hair caught back in a pony-tail and an earring in his right ear. He had a strong country accent quite unlike her father's flat Portsmouth voice and her mother's upmarket tones.

How solicitous of her he had been at the beginning! How kind! No one had ever been that kind to her before. Nothing had been too good for her. He'd made the fire and showed her how to cook in the open. He'd fed Nemo and currycombed him and given him water.

It hadn't lasted. After a few weeks he had said, 'How about you taking a turn?' And soon she had to chop the wood and make the fire and cook the food and make the beds and wash out the caravan – and only then had she been free to do what she wanted to do, which was to paint her pictures.

Chris had looked after the horse. That was the gypsy side of him. They all loved horses. He used to talk to the horse as though he was another human being. And he'd fondle him and even kiss him.

God she missed Chris!

Don't think about him then. Think about the wood.

Chop . . . chop . . . She piled the split logs against one of the caravan wheels.

'There,' she said out loud to herself. 'Now that'll last two days, and then I'll fetch some more.'

She felt a sudden sense of unease. She straightened up, turned and saw a man standing on the edge of her clearing watching her.

Chris? Chris?

A freezing hand closed over her heart.

But it wasn't Chris.

The morning was chilly, with cloud and pale sunshine which flared on the man's wire-framed glasses, hiding his eyes.

She took him in at a single glance: the old felt hat and the two coats held on with safety-pins and string, the old torn corduroy trousers, the old army surplus boots, the plastic shopping bag in each hand.

Gangrel.

The word leapt into her mind. She had come across it years before in a book of Scottish ballads and had looked it up. She still remembered some of its synonyms: outcast . . . tramp . . . vagabond . . .

The word itself was frightening. She felt a flutter of uneasy breathing in her ribcage.

The sun went behind a cloud and she could see his eyes, and his face became human. He wore a dirty beard, marked near the mouth with cigarette smoke, and his eyes were a slatey colour.

'Good-day to you, missus.'

117

His voice was whiney and heavily accented, a mixture, she thought, of Irish or Scottish and something else, but she wasn't sure what.

She stood by the caravan, the axe in her hand.

'You haven't got a bit of something, missus?'

'No.'

'A bit of bread. A bit of stuff.'

'I haven't anything.'

He took a few steps nearer.

'Fire's nearly out,' he said. 'Oh, yus.'

He put his hand in one of the plastic bags. She stepped back and raised the axe.

'See?' he said.

It was a tin of artichoke hearts.

'I'll swop you, missus. For a bit of bread.'

He looked harmless to Rachel.

'I'll give you a bit of bread,' she said. 'You wait over there where you are.'

She went into the caravan and looked for pieces of stale bread. When she came out he was on his knees in front of the fire puffing at the old embers. Soon, with a handful of twigs, he brought them to life.

'Got any coffee, missus?'

'That's my fire! Leave it alone!'

'A man must have coffee in the morning, missus. Oh, yus.'

'Were you here before?'

'Hereabouts.'

'Were you singing?'

'Singing?'

'Yes. Singing.'

'Sometimes I sings.'

It probably was him, she thought. He was simple. That was it. He was also old, probably in his sixties, and small – the two coats made him look bulkier than he was – and wizened and frail. There was nothing to fear from him.

'All right, let's have some coffee,' she said.

118

'Here.' He gave her the artichoke hearts. 'A woman gave them to me. Muck! I don't eat muck!'

She made coffee and gave him a mug. He dipped the dry bread into it and sucked it into a mouth that was devoid of teeth. She saw that his skin had the grey pallor of ingrained dirt and she decided to throw away the mug once he had gone.

'You got a horse, missus?'

'No.'

'Ain't going to get far without a horse.'

'I'm not going anywhere.'

'You need a horse for that there caravan. Oh, yus.'

'I had a horse. It went away.'

'I could get you a horse.' He tapped his nose. 'Contacts in the trade. What's your name, missus?'

'It doesn't matter. My husband's coming back in a minute. What's yours?'

He looked sly. 'Jackanory.'

'Is that your first name or your last?'

He laughed, hunching his shoulders and hugging himself. 'Neither. It's Rawley . . . Jackanory . . . '

It began to rain, a spring shower, but it was heavy for a short while. Rachel moved into the caravan. Rawley hunched by the fire, rain pouring off his felt hat. She couldn't let him stay there.

'Come in here in the dry.'

'Thank you, missus. Thank you.'

He sat opposite her on the other bunk. Chris's bunk.

'Nice place,' he said looking round. 'I could get you a good price for this. Contacts.' He put his hands to the stove to warm them. 'God made this stove. He made everything!' He swung his arm to indicate the caravan, the woods, the earth and sky. 'God made you. Are you ready for Him?'

Rachel was suddenly amused. The axe lay to hand. Rawley . . . Jackanory or whatever his name was, was even more fragile in close-up. She had nothing to fear.

'Yes, I'm ready for Him,' she said. 'Where are you travelling?'

'Cardiff. For my things. I left them there. My papers. Oh, yus.'

'What papers?'

He looked at her, his head on one side, a cunning expression on his face. 'That's for me to know and you to find out.'

'I don't care.'

'I'll tell you then. It's the Bible. I translated it.'

'You *what*?'

'They got it wrong. Through a glass darkly. That's wrong. Oh, yus. Through a dark glass. And lots more.'

He looked round vaguely. Most of his actions seemed to Rachel vague and unplanned.

Some of her early paintings were placed on the small dresser.

'Rabbits,' he said. 'Oh, yus. I know rabbits. Eaten them. In stews. Killed many a rabbit. Ain't seen no red ones though. Brown ones. Black ones. White ones. No red ones.'

'They're special,' Rachel said. 'Secret special.' Then the timbre of her voice changed and became almost childlike, and she said slowly, 'I'll tell you a story about Jackanory and now my story's begun . . . Do you like stories?'

'I loves stories . . . ' said Rawley, his eyes shining.

'This is a story about a little princess.'

'Oh, yus . . . '

'Once upon a time there was a little princess . . . '

' . . . little princess . . . ' he repeated, and then he put his arms around his body, hugging himself, and fixed his slatey eyes on Rachel.

' . . . who lived in a big house with her daddy and mummy . . . '

' . . . daddy and mummy . . . ' said Rawley.

'If you want to hear the story you mustn't interrupt.'

'No, no.'

'Well, anyway, they were rich and handsome and everyone

120

envied them. They were like people in a fairy tale; the king, the queen and the little princess.'

' . . . princess . . . '

'One night, when she was about six years old, the little princess was having a bath all by herself in the big bathroom in the big house. She often bathed herself because the king said she was a big girl – a big little princess really – and she must learn to bath herself.

'The king came into the bathroom and brought her a little yellow duck to play with and he played with it too. On top of the water and under the water in my lady's chamber . . . '

' . . . chamber . . . ' said Rawley, his eyes soft and shiny.

'Tickled her in my lady's chamber. And then he took her out of the bath and began to dry her . . . '

' . . . dry her . . . '

'He put her on his lap. And there was the red rabbit! The bunny. My bunny, the king said. Stroke my bunny. Isn't it a nice bunny? And the little princess stroked the king's bunny and the bunny was sick. Oops a daisy, the king said. The bunny loves you.'

' . . . loves you . . .

'And they did that often, sometimes in the bathroom and sometimes when the little princess had gone to bed. And as she grew older she became frightened of the red bunny. Very frightened. And she told her mummy even though her daddy had said, "This is our very biggest secret. And you are never to tell anyone."'

' . . . anyone . . . '

'And now my story's done . . . I'll tell you another about Jack and his . . . ?'

'Brother.'

'No, not brother. Mother.'

'What did the little princess's mother do?' asked Rawley.

'Her mother did nothing,' Rachel said. 'Nothing! And that's the whole point, isn't it? The whole fucking point!'

'I liked that,' Rawley said. 'Oh, yus. I liked it fine. Tell us another story, missus.'

Chapter 17

Time: 11.28 a.m.

Eddie Twyford driving the big Ford Granada, Macrae in front, Silver at the back.

Route: northbound on the carriageway across Hyde Park. Traffic fairly heavy.

'I think we're being followed, guv'nor,' Eddie said.

Neither detective turned.

Eddie flicked his eyes up to the rear-view mirror. 'Two cars behind us. Small white Mazda.'

Macrae reached up and repositioned the mirror.

'Where did we pick him up?'

'Not sure, guv'nor. I first saw him in the Buckingham Palace Road after we fetched Leo.'

'Can't see him.'

'He's still there.'

'OK, check him.'

There was a sudden surge of power as the big car gathered speed. Eddie pulled out, shot down the middle of the road to the consternation of both lines of traffic, barrelled through the Victoria Gate with the needle flickering on seventy.

There was a squeal of tyres and they were shooting across the Bayswater Road, round the Royal Lancaster Hotel, back on the Bayswater Road, and gunning the car west towards Notting Hill.

'Still can't see him,' Macrae said.

'About three cars behind.'

'Slow down, then. Can you see his index number?'

Silver was looking through the back window. 'The Mazda's turning off. Yeah, I got it.'

Macrae said, 'OK, go back to that underground car park in Queensway.'

They parked and Macrae told Eddie to radio the Mazda's index number through to the central computer then get himself a sandwich. He and Silver walked down Queensway.

'Eddie's getting to be an old woman,' Macrae said.

They walked in the direction of the park.

'You wouldn't think this was England,' he said.

Silver saw it through his guv'nor's eyes: the exotic restaurants getting ready for the lunchtime rush, the Arab and Indian shops, the newsagents where most of the dailies seemed to be in Arabic and German, French and Italian, the pavements jostling with Pakistanis, Indians, Bangladeshis, Hong Kong Chinese, Arabs from the Emirates, Malayans, Egyptians, Nigerians and Ghanaians, and little groups of myopic Japanese with cameras.

There were also some Brits.

Over it all hung a mixture of food smells. Silver could identify grilled kebabs, cardomom, curry, and sweet-and-sour. He could also smell the exhaust fumes of expensive cars.

'I like it,' he said.

'I didn't say I didn't like it, laddie. I said it didn't seem like England.'

They turned east along the Bayswater Road, walked about half a mile, entered a small tree-lined crescent and stopped in front of number seven.

It was a three-storey town house built in the nineteen sixties on land that had once been savaged by German bombs. It reminded Silver a little of Healey's house in Chelsea; every window was heavily barred, giving it the look of a fortress.

'This place is becoming an Arab ghetto,' Macrae said.

'For rich Arabs.'

'They're all rich. At least the ones who come to London are.'

Farther along the crescent, two stretched Mercedes were parked carelessly on the pavement while their uniformed chauffeurs chatted idly to each other.

Macrae pushed the bell at number seven. A doorphone speaker set into the wall at his elbow clicked into static and a man's voice said, 'Yeah? Who is it?'

'Detective Superintendent Macrae.'

'Who?'

Macrae said it again.

'What d'you want?' said the voice.

'I want to see Mr Howard Collins and I don't like standing on pavements talking to walls.'

After a moment the door opened a little way on a heavy chain and a hand came out. 'Let's see some ID.'

'You've been watching too much television,' Macrae said.

He held up his warrant card. The hand stretched for it but Macrae moved it slightly out of reach. 'Just read it. No need to feel. It's not in Braille.'

The door opened grudgingly.

'Mr Collins?'

'Yeah. I been expecting you.'

'That's nice,' Macrae said.

Howard Collins was a strange sight, Silver thought, even for this part of London. If he had been black and wearing a *kente* cloth, or brown and wearing a *djellabah* or his *jathika enduma* he would have looked natural. But he did not look natural. He was running now to fat but was still powerful-looking. He was in his fifties – trying to look twenty-five.

He had been using ex-President Reagan's age-reducing elixir, a hair dye. It had left some of his hair black but the roots grey. It was brushed forward on to his sunlamped forehead, once the home of a flourishing crop of acne. He was wearing a black silk shirt open to his navel and two gold chains round his neck. His trousers were also black and were stuffed into calf-length boots with polished steel toe-caps.

Behind him what sounded like a large party was in full swing.

He turned suddenly and shouted, 'Turn it down!'

The noise remained at the same level.

He said to Macrae and Silver, 'Hang on a sec.' They followed him to a large living room furnished in *hacienda moderne* – wrought ironwork, Moorish knick-knacks, leather pouffes, wall-tiles, floor-tiles, ceiling-tiles, potted pelargoniums.

A girl of about eighteen in a see-through short nightie was lying on the floor looking at the largest television screen either detective had ever seen.

'Poco silencio!' Collins shouted above the noise of the screen party.

'Que?'

The girl seemed hardly to hear him.

'Oiga! Juanita! Por favor, doll! Mas fucking silencio!'

He switched off the set.

There was a sudden, resounding silence. Juanita, dark, pretty in a sulky Latin way, looked at him as though he had trodden on something nasty and brought in on to the carpet.

'If you want to watch, go upstairs to the other set. Arriba! Mas television arriba.'

Juanita rose, stood for a moment backlit against the window while Silver and Macrae studied what she had on offer – which was of high quality – and then she marched out of the room.

'I dunno . . . ' Collins said. 'What did people like her do before the invention of TV?'

'Spanish?' Silver said.

'From Andalucia. Daughter of my gardener out there. Can't understand a bloody word of what's happening on TV but watches it all day and night. You know what they say about Spanish cooking: in the north they stew, in the centre they roast and in the south they fry – same with their women. Andalucian women are like fried chillies. Only not

125

so forward in the old brain box, if you get me. Sun's over the yardarm, you lads want a drink?'

'No thanks,' Macrae said for both of them.

'You can watch me, then.'

He poured himself a vodka and orange. 'OK, so what can I do for you?'

'You said you were expecting us,' Macrae said. 'Why?'

'Christ almighty. Robbie gets his head stove in. I'm his ex-partner. Why wouldn't I be expecting you?'

'Do you know a Mr Harris?' Silver said. 'Works at the Weyfo—'

'Weyford Marina. 'Course I know him. You been talking to him?'

'Just a little,' Macrae said.

'I get you. And what did Mr Curly Bloody Harris have to say?'

'Is that what they call him? Curly?'

'It's what I call him. You've seen his hair. So what did he say?'

'He said you had an affair with Mrs Healey. That Healey found out. That he brought in some heavies to correct the situation. That you ran off to Spain.'

For a moment Collins looked stunned. 'Hang on! Hang on!'

'You asked,' Macrae said.

'Anyway I didn't *run*. It wasn't like that.'

'All right. You made your way slowly to Spain. After that he bought you out.'

'So you say to yourselves, of course Collins's got a motive. Revenge for being beaten up.' He paused. Sweat was beginning to bead his forehead and glisten in the V of his throat. 'Listen, I know I've done some things . . . well, you know how it is in business . . . '

'We've never been in business,' Silver said.

'OK. Well, you skate on thin ice. Legalwise. That's what I'm getting at. But as far as Robbie goes, I mean not only him but anyone, well I could never, never do a thing like

126

that. It's not in me. And as for Shirley. Well, sure we did have something going but—'

'Why don't we start at the beginning, Mr Collins?' Macrae said. 'Then we'll know where we are. You were his partner. Tell us about that.'

'Sure you don't want a drink?' He poured himself another vodka and orange and lit a large Havana. 'Listen, Robson Healey and me, we go back a long way. Maybe I should say went back a long way – seeing as how he's deceased.'

They went all the way back to a secondary modern school in a bombed area of Portsmouth. Both their fathers had been killed in the war, both their mothers struggled to keep going.

'We used to do what a lot of kids were doing then, go through the bombed buildings for scrap. You could sell anything in those days, 'specially lead and copper. And when we didn't find the stuff in the broken buildings we used to nick it from anywhere. I remember once we stripped the lead off a church in Fratton. Took the bleedin' lightning conductor and all.

'I'm only telling you this so you'll know. I mean you asked. I don't want no bother about things that are past. OK?'

'OK,' Macrae said.

'We did what kids do, a little bit of shoplifting, little bit of nicking. That sort of thing. But even then Robbie was a hard man. Once – he couldn't have been more than eleven or twelve – there was this old busker playing the harmonica on the front at Southsea. Had his cap out on the pavement in front of him so the people could drop in coppers. Some old lady gives him a half-crown – a lot of money in those days – and Robbie says that's mine, oh no it ain't says the old punter and Robbie says I'll fight you for it. And he takes it out of the hat and the old chap must have seen that Robbie meant what he said because he didn't do anything.'

'Can we move on a bit?' Macrae said.

'Sure. But you did ask.'

'Tell us about the partnership.'

127

'You might say we was always partners.'

'You mean partners in crime,' Silver said. 'As the saying goes.'

'Yeah, yeah. You got it. But Robbie never wanted to be a . . . you know . . . '

'Criminal?' Silver said.

'Yeah. Criminal. He wanted money and power and respect but he wanted it where everyone could see it. Otherwise we'd just have gone on nicking things and ended up doing porridge.

'Anyway, Robbie cons me into putting up half the money for an old dredger. He'd got word on the grapevine that a big contract was coming up. Nothing had been done in Portsmouth or Southampton harbours during the war. And there'd been a hell of a lot of bombing so there was a hell of a lot of clearing up to do. Oh, and Robbie also took diving lessons and bought a proper diving suit so he could cut away underwater obstacles. I mean there wasn't nothing we couldn't do.

'We made a packet. Bought a second dredger and a floating crane. That's how we started. Then into coasters and when the oil boom began, into tankers. And when that went bust we managed to get out with a few quid and went into container ships.'

'Tell us about Mrs Robson,' Macrae said. 'Her relationship with her husband.'

'What about it?'

'She's the daughter of a judge.'

'You mean the other side of the tracks sort of thing? OK, it's a bit unusual but not all that rare. Society's changing.'

'So they tell me,' Macrae said, dryly. 'Go on.'

'She met him in the Med. She was in a party that chartered a yacht he owned. And you know how it is on a charter. I mean the hired help get to mix with the paying punters.'

'Spare us the social observations,' Macrae said. 'Just give us the facts.'

'OK, OK. Well, they fell in love. He was devastating

128

with women when he wanted to be. Good-looking and just dangerous enough to be around. It turned a lot of them on. It turned Shirley on. Mind you, it's never taken much to turn her on.

'Well, the marriage was OK for a while but then Robbie got itchy and started the old business with other women and Shirley got narked and when she protested he . . . well, he beat her up. I mean it didn't do to get narked with Robbie. He didn't like it.'

'He was a great man for beating people up,' Silver said.

'Yeah,' Collins said. 'You could say that. Anyway, she began to get more and more scared. And that's when she came to me. That's when that started.'

'On the boat?'

'On the boat. I also bought a cottage down there but that was too dangerous, so we didn't use it much. The boat seemed safe.'

'But it wasn't.'

'You might say that.' He fingered his mouth. 'Bridgework cost me thousands.'

'Not very friendly of an old pal.'

'Not very friendly putting a leg over his wife if it comes to that,' Collins said, thoughtfully.

'There was a daughter,' Silver said.

'Yeah, poor Rachel.'

'Why poor Rachel?'

'Well . . . I mean . . . Robbie and Shirley were never meant to be parents. The poor bloody kid lived a solitary kind of life. And there was her asthma as well. I really felt sorry for her. You know, they stuck her away in a boarding school. Hardly ever went to see her. And she used to be such a beautiful kid.'

'Beautiful?' Silver said, incredulously.

'You seen her? Well, you'll know then. That was another thing. Robbie and Shirley were a bloody good-looking couple. But when Rachel was a teenager she seemed to lose her looks. Don't think they forgave her.'

'They didn't have any more kids, then?' Macrae said.

'Well . . . ' he paused.

'He's dead. He can't send his heavies now.'

'It's not only that. Shirley and I . . . And anyway it's private. I mean she wouldn't want it known.'

Macrae said, 'Mr Collins, a man's been killed. His head was bashed in. A woman was seen leaving his house. But the murderer might have been a man. The blow was pretty hard. See what I'm getting at?'

'OK. I'm with you. A few years after Rachel was born, six or seven, Shirley got pregnant again. Told me she lost the baby but I always doubted it. I'd lay odds on an abortion.'

'Why would she do that?' Silver said.

'Christ, I dunno, mate. I'm not a bloody mind-reader. Maybe it's because of what I said: that she decided she wasn't so hot as a parent. It's only a guess, though.'

'Do you think she could have killed him?'

'I suppose anyone can do anything. But what for? I mean he'd made a big settlement on her when they separated. She wasn't short of a few bob.'

'What about Harris? He thinks Healey was still jealous of her having affairs with other men. That he thought of her as his possession.'

'Harris is just a bloody boatie.'

'But it could be true?'

He fingered his jaw again. 'Maybe. I alway wondered why they never divorced. Robbie was a great lad for what's mine's mine and what's yours is also mine. But never the other way round.'

130

Chapter 18

Macrae and Silver walked back to Queensway. Eddie had brought the car out from the underground garage and was leaning on a meter in the sunshine.

'Your lady called the switchboard,' he said to Leo. Eddie never called her Zoe or Miss Bertram, always 'Your lady'.

Leo looked concerned. There had been half a dozen explosive directives from the DI about taking private calls.

'Sorry, guv'nor,' Silver said to Macrae. 'I've asked her not to.'

Macrae nodded briefly. Since at least one ex-wife phoned him regularly about late payment of child support it was not really fair for him to comment.

'She said would you phone her? She has a clue pertaining to the case.' Eddie liked using phrases like that.

'Well, get on with it, laddie,' Macrae said. 'We need all the clues we can get.'

There was a payphone a few yards away and they watched him walk towards it.

'What about the Mazda?' Macrae said.

'Owned by a Mrs Purvis,' Eddie said.

'Any form?'

'Nothing.'

'I thought so. You're beginning to imagine things.'

Silver dialled Zoe's direct line. 'I asked you not to call the station.'

'Don't be such a grouch. I've worked something out. It may help.'

'What?'

131

'Erewhon is "nowhere" spelt backwards.'

'What do you want me to say?'

'Brilliant. Fantastic. Something along those lines.'

'What the hell is it supposed to mean?'

'Aah. You didn't ask that. It's not exactly backwards but nearly.'

'For God's sake! I'm standing in the middle of Queensway. Macrae's watching me and—' He distinctly heard background laughter. 'Are you having a party?'

'It's my going-away bash. You remember, we're going fishing.'

'Listen, I've got to go.'

'All right. Go. Leave me. Don't give it another thought. I supply you with a genuine clue and all you can say is "I've got to go." Well, let me remind you of what Thurber said, my friend, he said the claw of the seapuss gets us all in the end. And he's going to get you!'

'Are you drunk?'

'Never mind, Izaak Walton.'

'Goodbye.'

'Till we meet again . . . '

Silver went back to the car.

'Well? Have you solved it?' Macrae said.

Silver was embarrassed. 'It was nothing, guv'nor.'

'Don't be shy, laddie. I know Zoe. She wouldn't phone if it was nothing. And she's twice as bright as you.'

Eddie gave a snuffle.

'Well . . . all right . . . she says Erewhon is nowhere spelt backwards.'

Macrae stared at him uncomprehendingly. At last he said, 'So?'

'That's what I said.'

'Don't keep me in suspense, laddie.'

'The name on the daughter's caravan. In the forest.'

'What about it?'

'There was a wooden name-board. I thought you'd seen it, guv'nor.'

'And it said Erewhon?'

'That's right.'

'And you'd never heard of the word before?'

'No.'

'Not in three years at university?'

'No.'

Macrae gave a wintry smile. 'Christ knows what sort of place you went to. But never mind that now. Zoe's right. It *is* "nowhere" spelled backwards, or just about backwards. It's a famous bloody book by Samuel Butler. Never heard of him?'

'Never.'

'Nineteenth century. He was writing a satire on Utopia. That's why he called it Erewhon.'

'Meaning there's no Utopia anywhere. Nowhere.'

Macrae stared at Leo for a moment, then said dryly, 'Brilliant.' He turned to Eddie. 'I want to go up to Gospel Oak before we go back to the station.' He gave him the address.

Quick as a flash Eddie said, 'Sussex Gardens, then across the Edgware Road, left into Lisson Grove, then—'

'Why don't you go along Oxford Street and up the Tottenham Court Road instead of all these side streets and—'

'Oxford Street's usually jammed at this time, guv'nor.' Eddie's tone was stubborn.

'Oh, all right. But stop talking so much and let's get there.'

When they reached Gospel Oak Macrae said, 'I won't be long.'

The house was detached, with a garden that was large for London. Macrae opened the gate and went up the steps and rang the doorbell. He hadn't been here for a long time and noticed how upmarket the area had become. Artie had done well for himself.

It was more than twenty years since Macrae, then a copper on the beat, had first met Honest Arthur Gorman plying his illegal bookmaker's trade just off Piccadilly Circus in front of the Regent Palace Hotel.

In those days, before off-course betting was legalised, beat coppers were expected to fulfil an arrest quota on bookies in the same way as they were expected to haul in tarts.

Nobody liked it. Not the coppers, not the bookies and definitely not the tarts.

Macrae had now forgotten just how many bookies they were expected to arrest in a week but he would never forget his first meeting with Artie.

The difficulty was to get near the bookies to arrest them. They had runners and tick-tack men all up and down Piccadilly who could spot a copper a mile off.

So Macrae had borrowed an ice-cream cart, took out the big ice-cream drums and made a hidden nest for himself. His partner, in a white coat, wheeled the cart up Piccadilly and stopped it near Artie who was doing good business on the three-thirty at Brighton.

Suddenly Macrae leapt out and grabbed Artie before he could say, 'Nap!'

Artie paid his fine and was on the streets within twenty-four hours – which was standard – but the arrest had amazed him. He told the story to every East End punter he knew and Macrae became something of a legend.

Nor did Artie hold it against him, on the contrary he gained a great deal of kudos himself.

When off-course bookmaking shops became legal Artie expanded into a string of betting shops and he and Macrae kept up a desultory acquaintanceship.

Now the house door opened and Artie's wife said, 'Hello, George.' Behind her, in the shadows, Macrae could make out Stoker.

'Hello, Molly.'

She closed the door, put her arm around Macrae's neck and kissed him. 'Long time, George.' She patted his cheek. 'You're looking good.'

'So are you.'

It wasn't quite true. Her wide, good-looking face was thinner than he remembered and there were dark smudges under her eyes.

She was in her forties, a good fifteen years younger than her husband. She had blonde hair and might have been described as brassy except the word indicated hardness and Molly wasn't hard. He had always thought she had a lovely smile, guileless and genuine.

'You want to see Artie? He's in the garden room. Just go out, George.'

He went through the house, noting the expensive furniture: Honest Arthur Gorman had done very well for himself.

The garden room was nothing like the conservatory Macrae had been expecting but was a purpose-built office in the style of a Tyrolean hut.

'Hello, George,' Artie said as Macrae opened the door. 'Come on in.'

Artie was a foot shorter than Macrae and thin as a rail. He had lost his hair in his thirties and now looked like a bald ferret. His eyes were nervous and always on the move.

Macrae's eyes took in the room. There were three TV sets, a fax, four telephones, and a desk on which he could see the *Sporting Life* and the *Racing Guide*.

'What's all this?' he said.

'After I sold the betting shops I got so bloody bored Molly wouldn't let me in the house. You could say I'm a gamekeeper turned poacher.'

'Professional punter?'

'It passes the time.'

'Doing all right?'

'Lose a little, win a little. You know how it is. Sit down.' He waved to an expensive Thai bamboo chair.

There was a pause as the two men looked at each other. Macrae felt embarrassed. He had borrowed three thousand pounds for Susan's trip from Artie and now he found himself resenting him.

It had happened fortuitously. He had been turned down by

the bank and was on his way to his car when he'd bumped into Artie. They had had a drink and in the course of it Macrae, angry at the bank manager's attitude, had told Artie about it. The little bookmaker had taken out a roll of fifties the size of which made Macrae's eyes blink. He was about to start peeling off notes right there in the saloon bar, when Macrae had grabbed his hand and pushed it under the table.

'For Christ's sake, put it away!'

'George, believe me, and I'm not saying this to boast, but three thousand quid's not heavy for me these days. I've sold the business. Call it a loan. Pay me when you can.'

Macrae listened. He thought of his daughter. He thought of Linda. Where the hell was he going to get the money to pay for Susan's trip? A moment later he'd agreed and they'd gone to the lavatory and Artie had counted out sixty fifty-pound notes. It was a moment Macrae had regretted ever since.

'Stoker said you wanted to see me. If it's about the—'

'Hang on, George. I'd never have put it that way. Never! I said if you see Mr Macrae tell him if he's in the area to drop in and have a drink. I'll have to have a word with Stoker.'

'Why Stoker, Artie? He's not your speed. He's as thick as two planks and twice as nasty.'

'He's not a bad lad, George. Not really bad.'

'He's a villain. You know he broke a PC's arm in that last barney in Hackney. That's why he went down for so long.'

'Yeah. I know. But I need someone, George. For Molly, really. There's too many wide boys around now. No respect. I got a nice house. Nice things. I got money in the bank. They say why can't we have that? They don't think, he worked forty years for it and spent some time in the nick. They want it *now*. And that makes me worry.'

'But you've always sorted out that kind of dirt in the past.'

'I'm getting on, George. Sixty next birthday. Most of my old friends are dead or left the country. It's not a profession that encourages longevity.'

He paused and after a moment Macrae said, 'Well, here I am Artie. And if it's about the money—'

'It is, George.' He held up his hand. 'Just listen for a sec, all right? This is all part of what I've been telling you . . . I'm sick, George. I mean really sick . . . Cashing-in time . . . '

Macrae sat in silence unable to think of anything to say.

'Don't think I've given up. Not bloody likely. But when three specialists tell you to get your affairs in order then you bloody get them in order. Know what I mean?'

Macrae nodded.

'Now if any of these young buggers got wind of what was happening they might think I was a soft touch and go for Molly. Pick her up, hold her somewhere and bargain. And I don't want that. You know how I feel about Molly.'

'Of course I do. But Artie are you sure? I mean—'

'I told you. Three specialists. So anyway . . . let's not talk about that. Affairs, George. Getting them in order. That's what I want to talk to you about.'

'Artie, I know what you're going to say and I—'

'George, you haven't a clue what I'm going to say. I wanted to see you to tell you that I don't want that three thousand. That's what I wanted to tell you.'

'Artie, that's not—'

'Yes it is, George. I know you're a proud man and I don't want you to take it amiss. But it's the way I want it.' He smiled without humour. 'Last wishes and all that.'

Macrae felt a surge of emotion that was unfamiliar, uncontrolled feelings of the kind he had last experienced as a boy. He felt inadequate and for a moment hated Artie for making him feel that way. Inadequate . . . beholden . . . grateful . . . sad . . .

'I know what you're feeling,' Artie said.

'Do you?'

''Course I do. But you mustn't feel too bad. I told you when I lent you the money: three thousand isn't heavy for me. I've got enough . . . I was going to say to last me out but that's a joke. But enough to keep Molly in luxury. I'm sorry now we never had any kids. It would have been nice to have kids to leave something to. Anyway, that's all water under the whatsit. That's what I wanted to tell you, George. I just want you not to worry. If I thought you was a bent copper then I'd have asked for repayment. But you're something of a rare species. You give the rest of us something to think about . . . '

He looked at his watch and George saw that his face had gone grey. 'Pill time. Well, not quite but near enough. And after pill time, race time.' He got up. 'Good to see you, George. I still think of that ice-cream business. Still gives me a laugh. Don't forget us. And don't forget Molly.'

'Christ, Artie . . . '

'Don't, George.'

Macrae turned and walked across the lawn, through the house, thanking God Molly wasn't visible, down the steps and got into the car. Both Eddie and Silver noted his expression and kept their mouths firmly shut.

Chapter 19

Once upon a time there was a gangrel . . .
What's a gangrel, missus?
A vagabond.
Oh, yus.
Once upon a time there was a gangrel who walked the lonely roads, and along the rivers, and through the woods . . .
I love stories . . .
And his name was Rawley . . .
That's my name, missus!
It's a good name for you. Suits you. Good word too. I love words. Rawley . . . Jackanory . . .

In the Forest of Dean the weather had turned colder and clouds coming up from the south-west had darkened the sky. Occasionally there was a short rain-shower that passed over swiftly on a rising wind, causing the trees to clash overhead.

And one day Rawley, the gangrel, came to the Forest of Dean and there he met a princess.
Is that the princess who played with the red rabbit, missus?
Yes it is, and stop calling me missus. You can call me . . . let's see . . . Princess. Yes, you can call me that. Anyway the little princess grew up into a beautiful young woman . . .

They were in the caravan. She said, 'I don't tell stories for nothing, Rawley Jackanory. Everything has to be paid for.'

He looked anxious. 'But I ain't got money, missus. I mean Princess. Never carry it. Too dangerous. On the road there's thieves and murderers . . .'

'And gangrels . . . '

'And gangrels.'

'And reivers . . . and ruffians . . . '

The words made him afraid.

'Oh, yus.'

'Then you must work for your stories.'

She made him collect wood. She watched the bent figure make several trips into the undergrowth. When he had brought in enough she told him to saw it up then split it.

'Beautiful,' he said, looking at the saw. 'Ain't seen a saw like this for years. It'll spoil on rough work.'

'Use it.'

'And a lovely axe.' He rubbed the blade with his thumb.

'My husband loves his tools.'

He sawed up the logs and split them and soon there was a pile against the caravan that would last a week or more.

'Now can you tell the story?'

'What story?'

'About Rawley and the little princess.'

'First of all make the fire up. Princesses don't do work like that.'

He made up the fire and she heated two tins of beef stew which she had bought at the shop in Lexton. He ate his out of the tin with his own spoon. She wasn't going to give him one of hers. When he'd finished he wiped the spoon on the grass and tucked it carefully away in one of his pockets. All the time he ate he had watched her with his slatey eyes.

'Do you like secrets?' she said.

'Secrets? Oh, yus. And stories.'

She smiled. 'All right. I've told you one story, now I'll tell you another . . . about Jack and his . . . '

' . . . brother . . . '

'No!'

'About Jack and his mother?'

'No!'

'Who then?'

140

'About the little princess and how she met her prince and how they lived happily ever after.'

' . . . ever after . . . '

Again he placed his arms around his body and rocked back and forth.

Once upon a time there was a little princess who grew up to be very beautiful and was loved by everyone. One day she met a young man . . . a beautiful young man with a gold ring in his ear. He was a carpenter and he carried his carpentery tools wherever he went. But that was only a disguise for she knew he was really a prince. And he said to her if you kiss me on the lips and touch this gold ring in my ear you can have three wishes.

. . . wishes . . .

And so she kissed him on the lips and touched the ring in his ear and wished her first wish.

And he said, what is your wish?

And she said, I wish I could be loved by a prince forever and ever.

You are loved by a prince, he said.

For ever and ever?

And he said, There is no such time as forever. Do you want a second wish?

So she kissed him on the lips and touched the ring in his ear and he said, what is your second wish?

And the princess said I have been sick for many years. I want to be well for ever and ever.

And the prince said, you will be well.

For ever and ever?

And he said, There is no such time as forever. Do you want your third wish?

So she kissed him on the lips and touched the ring in his ear and he said, what is your third wish?

And the princess said . . . she said . . . my third wish is a very great wish . . .

What? What did the princess say?

The princess said, I wish someone would kill my father!
Oh God in heaven!

Goater's tart.

Macrae had said it first and it had stuck in Silver's mind. Hazy, a product of the movies. If he had been asked to describe her sight unseen it would have been some upmarket whore. Out of *Klute* perhaps. He would have been wrong.

It was early afternoon when they reached the house in Swiss Cottage, just a short drive from Artie Gorman's in Gospel Oak.

Here most of the houses had been sub-divided into apartments. But not the house belonging to Goater's tart. It was tall and elegant and brilliant white with a black front door and a shiny brass knocker.

The woman who came to the door fitted Silver's expectation perfectly. She was eighteen or nineteen, blonde, and looked like a Swedish tennis player.

'Mrs Spilsbury?'

'No. My name is Inge. Mrs Spilsbury fetches the children from school.'

She spoke languidly, the smoke from her cigarette curled up past her face and in the other hand she held a paperback novel.

Macrae identified himself and Silver and said, 'You live here?'

'I am the *au pair*.'

At that moment a large silver-grey Volvo estate pulled into the driveway and a woman of about twenty-seven, with two small children, got out.

'Here is Mrs Spilsbury,' said Inge.

Silver watched her come towards them. She was of middle height, with a wide face and high cheekbones. She was not as obviously pretty as the *au pair* but she was attractive. Silver had seen scores of women like Mrs Spilsbury waiting for their offspring outside kindergartens in the ritzier suburbs of London. In the vernacular, she was a sophisticated young mum.

Was *this* Goater's tart?

She came towards them, her eyebrows raised like two question marks.

The *au pair* said, 'They are from the police.'

The eyebrows rose further.

Silver thought she looked Slavic but her voice was English and educated.

'Have I been parking on the pavement?' She smiled but her eyes were hooded and her tone was crisp. 'Inge, would you take Sarah and Edward, please.'

Inge and the children disappeared into the house.

'Come into the drawing room.'

There was evidence of money everywhere, from the Persian rugs in the oak parquet hall to the pale peach Wilton in the drawing room, the modern teak furniture, the grey-green Chinese silk wall-hangings.

She seated them and said, 'Now what can I do for you?'

Macrae looked down at his notes. 'Mrs Lucy Spilsbury?'

'That does sound ominous.'

Macrae waited.

'Yes, I'm Lucy Spilsbury. What's all this about?'

Macrae said, 'Do you know someone called Lysander Goater.'

For one second she looked disconcerted then the mask slipped back and she said, 'Aaah. What about Mr Goater?'

'Is he a friend of yours?' Macrae said, picking his words carefully.

'You might say that.'

'Or a business acquaintance?'

'You might say that too.'

'Well, then you know what we've come about.'

'Healey,' Mrs Spilsbury said.

'Robson Healey,' Macrae said.

'I think I knew that something like this might happen sooner or later. Not murder but something unpleasant.'

'It was a chance you took.'

'A chance.'

'What happened?' Macrae said.

She looked towards the door as though to make certain it was closed against listening ears.

'Nothing *happened* in that sense. It had all happened. I mean—' For a moment, as she cast her mind back, her brittle exterior seemed to soften and bend.

Silver realised Macrae was taking it too fast. If he pushed her, Mrs Spilsbury would start yelling for her lawyer. He said quickly, 'You have a lovely house.'

Silver could feel Macrae's hostility but ignored it.

Lucy Spilsbury said, 'And two lovely children. And I aim to keep them and it. I'm looking for a deal.'

'This isn't *LA Law*,' Silver said.

'Isn't what?' Macrae said, baffled.

'I'm not the assistant DA,' Silver went on. 'We don't do deals.'

'Everybody does deals. The world's built on deals. That's something I've learned the hard way.'

Macrae said, 'What sort of deal?'

'I tell you what happened and you keep me out of it – at this stage anyway – until you make an arrest or it comes to trial. And then we change the situation slightly. Otherwise I ring a lawyer. Now.'

'In what way slightly?' Macrae said. 'And why the deal?'

'Why the deal? Because I'd never work again, not for Mr Goater. And I need, Mr Goater. I need the top drawer, not a quickie against the wall down at King's Cross. You see, before my husband was killed in a crash a couple of years ago we had a good life. All this.' She indicated the house. 'He was making a lot of money in the City. I'd never been trained for anything. Then suddenly – bang! The phone rings. They tell me about the smash. Not that he's dead, you understand, but that he's been injured. That was to prepare me. I said how bad? And they said very bad. Very, very bad. And then I knew.'

144

Neither Macrae nor Silver spoke.

'They say life stops. Well, it doesn't. I had to fetch the kids from school, see that they were told and fed and that they bathed and washed behind their ears. That helps, of course. But it doesn't pay the rent.'

'How did you get on to Goater? A contact magazine?'

'Mr Goater doesn't advertise. Certainly not in contact magazines. He's exclusive. No, I knew that there had to be someone like Mr Goater because after I left school one of my friends needed money and she found herself a Mr Goater. That was some years ago, but she knew the route.'

'You could have sold the house,' Macrae said.

'Have you tried selling a house recently? Don't make me laugh. In this part of London you can hardly see out of your windows for For Sale boards.'

'So you decided on the carriage trade,' Silver said.

Lucy Spilsbury turned and gave him a slightly cynical smile. She had magnificent teeth.

'That's right,' she said. 'The carriage trade. And compared to some boardroom takeovers in the City it's clean and decent.'

'Who are these people?' Macrae said, unamused.

'Mostly businessmen. Mostly from abroad.'

'I thought they brought blow-up dolls.'

She didn't bother to comment. 'The Japanese are the easiest. They don't talk much. And they pay on the nail. Most are lonely, far from home, terrified of AIDS. I try to talk to them on their level. Which is more than the average bimbo can offer – and probably their wives as well. By the time I go and see them I've read that day's *Financial Times* and *Wall Street Journal* and I know what the markets are doing, what the Hang Seng Index is standing at and the Australian All Ordinaries. In other words, I've done my homework.'

'But you don't chat about the Stock Exchange all the time,' Silver said.

'There was always the "entertainment".'

'Is that what it's called these days?' Macrae said.

'It's what I called it. That's what they were getting. I don't pretend otherwise.'

'Tell us about the entertainment at Robson Healey's house.'

She'd had a call from Goater before lunch on Sunday. She'd been to Healey's house before. She didn't particularly like him but didn't dislike him either.

'What about his proclivities, if any?' Silver asked.

She smiled again, the eyes widening, the teeth showing white and shining, the rather ordinary face transforming itself into something quite different.

'Proclivities,' she said. 'What a lovely word. No, he didn't have any proclivities. I think I was a wife surrogate. We'd usually have a drink. Go out to dinner. Come back to his house. It was civilised.'

'Then the entertainment? Or was that before?'

'No. After dinner.'

'So what about Sunday?'

'I got there around six. I'm not absolutely sure of the time. I rang but no one came to the door. I tried it and it was open. It didn't surprise me. It had happened before when he was expecting me.

'When he wasn't in the drawing room I went to the bedroom. He was on the floor. Dead or dying I didn't know which. I didn't stay long enough to find out. All I knew was I had to get out of the place.'

Macrae said, 'So you ran.'

'Yes, I ran.'

'What were you wearing?'

'A white blouse. Black trousers. Black high-heeled shoes. Not much good for running.'

'And carrying a bag,' Silver said.

'It had my make-up in it and a nightgown. He wanted me to stay the night. How did you know about the bag?'

'You were seen,' Silver said.

She looked down at her hands. 'I don't often panic. I don't even like the word. I don't like people who get flustered.'

146

'But that flustered you,' Macrae said.

'I panicked.'

'And then?'

'Drove around for a while and then I came home. There were spots of blood on my blouse. God knows how they got there. I never went up to him. So I cut it up and burnt it. I think I knew . . . that it was only a matter of time before you gentlemen arrived.'

Chapter 20

'She was the one old Lady Hickson saw,' Macrae said. 'So that means there must have been someone before her. Someone who came and went while the old girl was asleep. She said she'd dropped off, remember?'

'That's if you believe Spilsbury, guv'nor.'

'Can't think why she'd lie. Don't see any motive, do you, laddie?'

Eddie said, 'What number?'

Silver told him and he began to slow down.

'That's the block over there,' Silver said, pointing to the mansion flats where his parents lived. He had taken the opportunity, while they were in north London, to ask Macrae if he could drop in and tell his mother and father of his changed holiday plans.

The plans had become somewhat truncated, a fact which Zoe did not yet know.

He had wanted to postpone the holiday because of the Healey murder but when he mentioned it Macrae had said, 'You haven't had a holiday for a year. You're no bloody good to me if you become stale. Anyway, I can get Geddes to help me on this.'

Jack Geddes, a thrusting detective sergeant who'd come out top of his year at the training college, was younger than Silver, and Leo was unhappy at the thought of Geddes stepping into his shoes and working with his boss.

So he had argued with Macrae and the new arrangement was that he would go to the Wye for the weekend and if the investigation hadn't closed, he'd come back and work on it until it was finished before taking the remainder of his leave. He was not thrilled about the prospect of telling Zoe this.

'There's always the possibility he started getting rough with her,' Silver said, returning to the Spilsbury–Healey 'entertainment'.

'People have wenches not wrenches lying around a bedroom, laddie. It was brought in as a weapon. Anyway, she'd been to Healey before. She wouldn't have gone if she'd been expecting rough stuff.'

'I admire her, in a way.'

'I bet you do.'

'No, not in that way. Well . . . in that way too, I suppose. No, I mean, it must have been hard with two kids—'

'And a large house, and an *au pair*, and a private school. Jesus Christ, she wouldn't give up a bloody thing.'

'Well, Mrs Thatcher started it, guv'nor. It's called the "enterprise culture".'

Eddie began to squeeze the car into what would have been a non-existent parking space for the average motorist.

'What sort of deal could we offer?' Silver said.

'We just let her change the nature of the visit,' Macrae said. 'Nothing difficult about that. She was going to see him. Half a dozen reasons. Doesn't matter *why* she was there. Saw him lying in a pool of blood. Panicked. Ran. I don't mind what bloody reason she gives for being there, just so long as she tells *us* the truth. We're not finished with her yet.'

'I won't be a minute,' Silver said, getting out of the car and entering the block of flats.

As the little cage lift reached the top floor he could hear the piano in his father's music room and his resonant voice counting, 'Vun-and-two-and-three-and-four-and— Quavers, Futterman, quavers!'

As Leo entered his mother said, 'What's this? A visit from my big son on a working day!'

She too had trouble with the English voiced 'w' and it came out 'vurking day'.

'I was nearby,' Leo said. 'I came to say goodbye again

and tell you I'm not going to be away for a week. Only for a couple of days.'

'But darling, you need a holiday,' Lottie said. 'Sit. Sit.'

'I can't.'

'Have you had your lunch?'

'I'll get something at the station.'

'What can they give you at the station? Plastic rubbish. Have a sandwich. A piece of cake.'

'Mr Macrae's waiting for me in the car.'

Her face fell but her natural hospitality overcame her antipathy to the man. 'Fetch him, darling. I make some coffee.'

'I don't think he'll—'

'Has he had his lunch?'

'No.'

'This is your mother speaking. Go fetch him.'

Leo went down to the car and said, 'My mother insists you come up for a coffee, guv'nor. What about you, Eddie?'

But Eddie shook his head. 'I had mine. I'll take a nap.'

'I could do with a coffee.' Macrae followed Leo into the building.

Lottie had met Macrae several times and she and Manfred had early formed an unfavourable opinion of him. Manfred believed that men who lived without wives were probably not as clean as they might be.

Once, at a small Christmas party given by the Silvers, Macrae had arrived well oiled and had used the bathroom.

A moment later Manfred went in, checked, and then looked for and found Leo. 'He hasn't washed his hands,' he said.

'Who?'

'Your Mr Macrae.'

'Dad, for God's sake!'

'I checked the towels.'

'You want me to ask him?'

'I just want him to wash his hands when he goes to the toilet.'

'I'll tell him, Dad. I'll tell him he's got to wash them in antiseptic.'

'Don't be smart with your father. You know what I mean.'

On the other hand Lottie saw him as a kind of albatross around Leo's neck; someone who was in a constant state of war with the police hierarchy and who would therefore do her son no good.

But no one would have known that, for her greeting was warm and gracious – the doctor's daughter from Vienna.

'A little Bismarck herring,' she said. 'A little salad.'

Macrae said, 'Please don't go to any trouble, Mrs Silver.'

'What trouble?'

As she spoke she laid things out on the coffee table in the drawing room.

There was the noise of raised voices in the music room, then a door slammed and a spotty-faced youth with large ears, thick glasses and a flushed face passed the drawing-room door on his way out.

They heard Manfred's voice carry down the corridor, 'Vun-and-two-and-three-and-four-and! You hear me? Count!' The front door slammed.

Manfred came into the drawing room. 'My God!'

'You remember Mr Macrae,' Leo said hastily.

'Certainly I remember Mr Macrae.'

Manfred looked dapper in a bottle-green corduroy jacket, his grey hair and Van Dyke beard were glossy and well combed. He kept his hand firmly in his pocket in case Macrae tried to shake it.

'Just a little lunch for Mr Macrae and Leo,' Lottie said.

He sat down and watched his son and his son's superior officer tuck into the Bismarck herring and salad.

After a moment he said, 'Futterman!'

'What, Dad?'

'Two days ago Arnold Futterman called me up. You remember Futterman?'

'Wasn't he a plumber?'

'Now plumbing supplies. Has a shop in Finchley. Gold taps. Teak toilet seats. Sells to Uppies. They tell me he's going to be a rich man.

'So anyway Futterman calls me and says his son Harold is taking his exams and he would like that I give him a polish. A little Debussy, a little Bach, a little Schubert. I said, "Arnold, I got pupils booked from now till Christmas. I got more pupils than I can handle."'

He absently reached for a dill pickle and began to chew it.

'You know what he says to me? He says, who came out one night in the snow to mend a burst pipe? Who came out to unblock the lavatory that time Leo stuffed—'

'Manfy!' Lottie said. 'People are eating! Not about lavatories!'

'So anyway Futterman says I owe him. So what can I say? You owe someone, you owe him.' He pointed to the music room. 'That was Harold Futterman you just heard. Thirteen years old. Spots. I ask him to play some Bach. So he plays for me the F sharp minor prelude from the second book. I said you're playing it too fast. It's marked *andante*. He says Glen Gould plays it fast. I said: "Harold, Glen Gould is dead from playing so fast."'

He turned abruptly to Macrae. 'Do you play the piano?'

'I used to play the drum,' Macrae said.

'Ah. A tympanist. I too. Rataplan! Rataplan! In an orchestra here in north London. Maybe you heard of it.'

'I don't think Mr Macrae would've—'

'Why not? People came from all over. We played at the old Hippodrome in Golders Green. I remember once in Haydn's 'Drumroll' symphony—'

'In a band,' Macrae said, fearing he was getting deep into unchartered territory.

'Ah. A band. Gene Krupa. Big Sid Catlett. I remember the old V-discs. From the war. American All Stars.'

'A cadet band,' Macrae said. 'The school cadet band.'

Manfred stared at him. Silence fell. Leo hastily tried to fill it.

'What are you up to, Dad? How's the symphony coming along?'

'He's got a new idea, your father. Now an opera.'

'The biggest opera ever staged,' Manfred said. 'Bigger than *Aïda*. Bigger than *The Trojans*.'

'What's it about?' Leo said.

'Better you don't ask,' Lottie said.

'Luther. The Reformation. The Diet of Worms.' He turned to Macrae. 'With music worked from Bach's church cantatas. *Ich habe genug . . . Wachet Auf . . .* Full of irony, don't you think?'

Macrae stuffed a piece of herring into his mouth so he would not have to reply.

'Sounds fantastic,' Leo said.

'Fantastic is right,' Lottie said. She turned to Macrae. 'Tell me, Mr Macrae, how is Leo doing?'

'For God's *sake*, mother!'

'I mustn't ask about my only son? We're interested. Have I made a mistake?' She turned fierce eyes on Macrae.

'No, no, Mrs Silver. Of course not. He's doing well.'

'There . . . ' Mrs Silver said to Leo. 'Did that hurt? Now we know.'

The sweat had burst out on Leo's face and trickled down to his chest.

As they got into the car he said, 'I'm sorry about that, guv'nor.'

'Sorry about what?'

'Putting you through it. My family is—'

'Laddie, you don't know when you're well off.' Macrae's expression was bleak.

'Where to now, guv'nor?' Eddie said.

'Let's go and bully Mrs Robson Healey,' Macrae said. 'It's about time we did.'

* * *

153

Rawley . . . Rawley . . . Jackanory . . . How does your garden grow?

You can't stay here all the time, the princess had said. Not in the caravan. It wouldn't be right.

He went under. Like a dog.

Rawley . . . a dog's name . . .

If I had three wishes . . . I wish . . . I wish . . .

But there was nothing he could think of to wish for.

It was gloomy afternoon now in the Forest of Dean with the trees like witches and light rain on the wind. Rachel had thought to send him away but emptiness and loneliness changed her mind. He would leave a vacuum where only she remained. He gave the same companionship as a dog. He wanted stories like dogs want stroking. No, not a dog, a child. A sixty-year-old child who wants to hold back the dark. Just one more story, Mummy . . .

She had done it herself, wanted to postpone going to bed for ever in case he came in, bringing the red rabbit with him.

So she told Rawley he could go in the dry under the caravan. Preserve the proprieties. 'I'm not sending you away,' she had said when she saw his face. 'You can come in again when I'm not resting. You can't be here when I'm in bed. My husband wouldn't like it.'

'No. No. Not in here. I know that.'

So he lay in a blanket with his plastic bags alongside him, listening to her movements above. She wasn't resting. She was pulling things and pushing things. And sometimes he heard her voice. Not what she was saying, but the series of strange glottal sounds that made him think of rage.

He was a gangrel.

He was afraid.

Oh, yus.

Chapter 21

It was early evening in central London, the ancient brickwork glowing in the late sunshine.

Zoe and Leo were sitting at their usual table in the Old Vienna off The Strand, one of the few wine bars she would patronise. It was her contention that most food offered in wine bars, pubs and restaurants came out of a single gigantic kitchen in Swindon: all those veal chasseurs and marengos, that deep-fried Camembert, the chilli con carnes – all cooked in steaming vats, then frozen, loaded into trucks and aimed at a million microwaves the length and breadth of the land.

In the Old Vienna the cooking was sound if not brilliant and sometimes tasted slightly burnt – which she defined as a genuine flavour – and the wines were dependable.

'So what's all this in aid of?' Zoe said.

'All what?'

'Glasses of plonk.'

She was still slightly high, he thought, from her lunchtime party, though he had established that it was not a going-away bash for her holiday but because a new client had sent in a case of champagne. The holiday was something he was approaching slowly.

They were sitting in a bay window with the sun streaming in and he thought she was looking stunning in black and red; his favourite combination. He loved looking at her face with its high cheekbones, the red slash of colour on the lips, her olive skin. She was wearing stockings and a mini skirt and the sun caused her legs to shine.

'OK,' Zoe said. ' "My Day, by Leopold Silver. Boy Detective." '

He laughed and told her about Collins then Mrs Spilsbury and calling in to see his parents, but not the reason. And then the second visit to Shirley Healey.

'Oh, right. The wife.'

'She must have been beautiful once. Cool. Laid back. Except the phrase apparently means something different to her.'

'Leo, I think you're meeting the wrong class of person.'

He had hardly recovered from Mrs Spilsbury's smile with its promise of hidden vice, when he was under the cool eyes of Shirley Healey whom he knew to be far from cool.

Ladies' legs were what undid Silver. Legs in shiny stockings. Mrs Healey wore shiny stockings and had long legs which she crossed. Last time she had worn a black dress in deference to her abruptly deceased husband, but when they had interviewed her an hour earlier she was wearing a white polo-neck sweater which showed off her colouring to perfect advantage.

She'd let them in as though she had been expecting them and her expression was wary. They'd perched on the same button-backed chairs they'd sat in the first time and she had sat in a low chair facing them.

'We've spoken to Mr Harris,' Macrae began. The tone of his voice was brisk, no nonsense.

'I thought you might.'

'And Mr Collins.'

Her eyes widened. 'I thought he was in Spain.'

'No, he's in London. Has Mr Harris been in touch with you?'

'He phoned to say you'd been to the cottage. He's the caretaker.'

Macrae frowned at her. 'That's it? The caretaker?'

'How else would you describe someone who looks after your property in your absence?'

'It's not what he does in your absence that we're talking about. But in your presence.'

156

'What has he been suggesting?'

Very cool, Silver thought.

'That you and he were, are, lovers.'

She made a slight grating noise that might have been a laugh. 'That's absurd.'

Silver said, 'He says that last weekend you and he had a party that occupied Saturday and Sunday.'

'Mr Harris has a vivid imagination. The only relationship I have with Mr Harris is one of employer and employee.'

'What about the champagne? There were empty bottles in his boat as well as in your cottage.'

'How would I know?'

'The champagne was vintage and expensive,' Macrae said. 'It isn't the kind of thing he would normally drink.'

'I'm not responsible for what people drink.'

'The same brand was found in your cottage.'

'Inspector, I find this impertinent.'

'Superintendent!'

She waved a hand. 'Whatever.'

'Mrs Healey, let's not mince words.' Macrae's voice dropped two semi-tones and became darker. At this point Silver began to feel sorry for her. 'You say Harris is a caretaker; he says you are lovers; that you and he have drinking bouts; that you go to bed together.'

'You have a gift for phraseology.'

'I inherit it from a Presbyterian grandfather.'

It was no use being ironic with Macrae, Silver thought.

'And you believe him?' she said. 'Why on earth do you think I would be interested in a person who looks after boats?'

Macrae said softly, 'You were interested in Robson Healey. It might be said that a man who owns and charters a yacht "looks after boats".'

She lit a cigarette and Silver caught a slight tremor in her hand as she did so. He suddenly imagined the nerve storm that must be convulsing her brain.

157

'You had an affair with Howard Collins. And *he* looked after boats. I'm using the phrase loosely. It does seem that you have an interest in men who deal with boats.'

'That's pure coincidence,' she said.

'But you did have an affair with Collins?'

'My husband was having a string of affairs, several simultaneously. I needed someone . . . to give me back my self-esteem . . . I needed someone to . . . cherish and be cherished by.'

The thought of anyone being cherished by Howard Collins made Silver blink. 'Cherish?' he said.

'Love is too strong a word. I didn't want to love Mr Collins nor did I want him to love me.'

'Does love frighten you?'

'Don't be silly! Of course not. What I'm saying is that when something like that happens . . . I mean when one's husband goes off with another woman, there's a vacuum. One needs to fill it.'

'But you did have someone who could have filled it and given you love and whom you could have loved,' Macrae said.

Mrs Healey drew heavily on the cigarette. 'You mean Rachel?'

'Yes, Rachel.'

'I don't want Rachel brought into this!'

'Why is that?'

'Because I don't. She has nothing to do with anything. She lives her own life.'

'Did you ever love her? Macrae said brutally.

She looked down at the cigarette. 'My relationship with her is private.'

Silver abruptly took her off on another tack. 'Have you a photograph of your husband as a young man?'

'I suppose so.' She rose and went over to a rose-wood cabinet and began to rummage in one of the drawers.

Macrae scowled at Silver for interrupting the flow but

158

Silver pretended not to notice. One thing he had learned from Macrae's frontal interrogation method – rather like a siege gun – was that it was sometimes better to go off at tangents, change the subject, the pace, the thrust – and throw the person off guard.

'It was taken about fifteen years ago,' she said.

Silver saw a man he realised most women would have found good-looking; dark-haired, his face framed by the heavy sideboards that were fashionable in the early seventies. He was standing in the shallow end of a swimming pool with the water up to his waist. The top half of his body was well made, hairy, and powerful. On his shoulders, naked, was a little girl, snub-nosed and pretty. He was laughing and the picture would have been a perfect family snap but for the expression on the child's face. It had a bleakness and an unhappiness which touched Silver immediately.

'Rachel?' he said.

She nodded. She must have been five or six.'

Silver passed it to Macrae then said matter-of-factly, 'Did she like the water?'

'Loved it.'

'She doesn't seem to be enjoying herself.'

Mrs Healey compressed her lips.

Macrae said, 'Did you have any other children?'

'No. Only Rachel.'

'Was there any reason?'

'I don't see that's any of your business.'

'Was your marriage already breaking down by the time Rachel was born?'

'It happened afterwards.'

'Did it have anything to do with Rachel?'

'God damn it! I've told you over and over, don't bring Rachel into this. She's had enough to put—'

'Go on.'

She shook her head.

'Were you afraid of your husband?' Silver said.

159

'What?'

'Were you afraid of him?'

'Was he a violent man?' Macrae said.

'Did he ever attack you?' Silver asked.

'Beat you up?'

Her head began to move from side to side like a stunned boxer avoiding punches.

'I don't know what you—'

'It's quite simple,' Silver said. 'Was he rough with you? Did he ever hit you? Attack you?'

She stubbed out the cigarette and her hand was shaking so much Silver thought she might not be able to find the ashtray.

Macrae said brutally, 'Have you ever had an abortion?'

'How dare you!' Her pale complexion had become chalky.

Macrae said, 'If you did have an abortion after the Abortion Act made it legal and if you had it at any of the registered clinics under your married or maiden names, we'll find out. Why don't you make it easier for all of us?'

She took another cigarette from an inlaid box on the table in front of her. Silver picked up her lighter and lit it for her.

'Yes, I did.'

'When was that?'

'Six or seven years after Rachel was born.'

Silver made a note.

'Why?' Macrae asked.

She leaned forward and covered her face with her hand. Silver thought she might be hiding tears but he was wrong. Almost wearily she looked up at them and said, 'It seemed like a good idea at the time.'

'Did your husband know?'

She shook her head. 'He was in Japan on business. He was away for six weeks. I didn't tell him.'

Macrae said in a softer voice, 'You were terrified of him, weren't you, Mrs Healey?'

She nodded slowly.

160

'Is that why you were never divorced?'

She looked up at them and then said slowly, 'He said if I took him to court he'd kill me.'

'And you believed him?'

'Oh yes. I believed him all right.'

In the Old Vienna Zoe sipped her wine then said, 'But why? Why did he threaten to kill her?'

'I don't know. Macrae thinks it's because she knew too much about his business affairs. He and Collins were a right pair and he didn't want lawyers poking about. Both Collins and Harris say Healey was obsessively possessive. The point is she was terrified of him. And so was Rachel. She as good as told us. So I'm going to do a bit of probing.'

'When?'

'Tomorrow?'

'Wait one little minute, sport. Tomorrow we start our holiday.'

'This is on the way. We'll just—'

'Leo. You said no work. You said—'

'I know . . . I know . . . '

'Anyway, you've always told me that you were either on duty or off, no half measures. And that when you're off duty you have no insurance and no back-up.'

He told her about Jack Geddes. 'I don't want some bloody whizz-kid taking over my place with Macrae. I want to come back with something, and it's only going to take an hour or so. Everyone seems to have forgotten Rachel's husband Chris. But I've got a kind of feeling about him. And I want to check it out. We stop in Wiltshire. I ask him a few questions. Then on to the Wye.'

'You promise.'

'I promise.'

'You swear on St Bartholomew's Holy Ear?'

'I swear.'

'Say it.'

He said it. Someone at the bar laughed.

161

'OK,' Zoe said. 'That's a terrific oath. I can't tell you all the things that'll go wrong if you break it.'

'I'm not going to break it. We'll be at Paxham by lunch-time.'

'Leo, is it going to be nice?'

'The holiday? Of course it's going to be nice!'

'I mean the village. And the pub. I've never stayed at a pub before. Shouldn't we have booked into a hotel instead?'

'The Paxham Arms is in the guide book. It gets a star.'

'But the food might be Swindon.'

'The food gets a star too.'

'What about the beds?'

'The accommodation also gets a star.'

'What if it's too far from anywhere?'

'Look, we're going on a fishing holiday, OK? Anyway, Hereford's only about twelve miles away.'

'Terrific! Known far and wide for its . . . cattle. Swinging Hereford! I've always wanted to go there. A week watching the cattle, and you throwing your rod or line or whatever into the water is going to be just dandy.'

Silver ran his tongue over his lips. 'Well, you're in luck. It just might not be a week.'

'What?'

'Not a whole week.'

'OK, I can live with that. How much of a week?'

'Part.'

'What sort of part?'

'The smaller part.'

'How long?'

'We've always wanted to go away for a weekend haven't we? A weekend in the country! We've talked about it often.'

'Leopold,' she said in a dangerous voice. 'I think we should have a little chat. I'll do the chatting . . . '

Chapter 22

Linda Macrae watched the early-evening news on television. Sometimes she saw George when he was working on a case. Soon after he had left her and gone to live with 'the other woman' as she still sometimes thought of her, she had seen him on the six o'clock news and had been filled with a rage so great that she was frightened by its unfamiliarity.

But that had passed.

His name was often in the papers investigating this or that. She could read it now without anger. She used to dream about him a great deal. In some of her dreams he had come back to her and they were living together again.

She wished now she had not had to go to him for the money for Susan's trip, but there had been no other way. It had seemed to give him the idea of coming back into her life. Once, she would have given anything to have him back. Not now. She had won her right to her own life by living through a thousand lonely nights and ten thousand lonely meals.

It was George who was lonely now.

She decided to have a drink, make herself supper and then read. There was not much to watch on television and in any case she was suspicious of the medium, scared of becoming dependent on it now that Susan was no longer around. When the two of them had lived together the TV had been on much of the time, a kind of visual muzak.

No, she would read. The thick paperback edition of *Middlemarch* had been frowning at her from her bookcase for months. It was one of the novels she had tried to read during her self-improvement phase and which had defeated her. Every time she looked at it she felt guilty. She would try to get past the first forty to fifty pages and into the story proper.

She was pouring herself a glass of wine when the phone rang. For a second she felt a faint increase in her heart rate. David had said she should call him if she wanted to go out to dinner and she had decided that she didn't and wouldn't – and was regretting it. This might be him now. But it wasn't.

'Hello, George,' she said.

She could hear the sound of clinking glasses and voices and knew he was in a pub.

'How are you?' he said.

'Fine.'

'I was wondering . . . ?'

'Yes?'

'I thought I'd come over.'

'Is something wrong?'

'Just a chat. About Susan.'

'But we had a chat the other night. There's no more news, George.'

'You know what I mean. A talk. Like we used to have.'

'When was that?'

'Well . . . you know . . .'

'George, we haven't had a chat in that sense for twenty years.'

'Well . . . I miss them.'

'Do you?'

'What about you?'

'I haven't thought about it.'

'Is that all right then?'

'What?'

'Me coming over.'

'No, it isn't. I'm going out to dinner.'

Pause.

'Out?'

'People do go out, you know. I mean ex-wives are allowed out.'

'With him?'

164

'If you mean David, yes.'

'Is it David now?'

'George, for God's sake! You don't think I'd have someone to supper in my flat and call him Mr Leitman, do you?'

'Where are you going?'

'I don't know. I'll leave that to him.'

'Do you like him?'

'Really, George, don't be absurd. I hardly know him.
Anyway, its nothing to do with you.'

'I don't know what you see in him.'

'I don't *see* anything. He's a man who lives upstairs. I'm
pleasant to him, he's pleasant to me. We meet on the stairs.
We share the same house. He's had supper with me once. I
don't owe you explanations.'

'I mean, he's just a bloody writer.'

'That's right, George. Just a bloody writer.'

'Writing about the police!'

'I thought that would get you.'

'How do you mean?'

'That's your territory, isn't it? The police.'

'All that rubbish about enclosed societies.'

'You just don't like people trespassing, do you?'

'Well, why doesn't he write something he knows about?'

'I suppose he knows about the police.'

'Och, you know that's nonsense. How could he know about
the police? No one knows about coppers unless they've been
one.'

She thought of several examples she could have quoted
which would have countered that argument but suddenly
she felt her energy seep away. She just couldn't be bothered
arguing with him.

'When will you be back?' he said.

She considered the possibility of George arriving at midnight and said, 'I don't know. And if you were thinking of
coming over – don't.'

'You were never like this.'

'Like what?'

'You never really cared about men.'

'What?'

'Little Linda Brown's come a long way.'

'I'm not having any more, George. Don't phone me up if you're going to say things like that.'

'Are you sleeping with him?'

'Goodbye, George.'

She put the phone down. She was shaking with anger. Little Linda Brown! Once she had tried to explain to George what had happened to her since she had been on her own, tried to make him understand that twenty years of making her own decisions, mapping out her own life, had changed her.

But change was something he could never get to grips with. He didn't like change. It disturbed him. And she knew that the Metropolitan Police had changed out of all recognition since he had joined. He was being left behind. He should have been a detective chief superintendent or even a commander by now. But he was like a dinosaur trapped in a world that was slowly growing colder.

She reached for the phone, dialled.

'Hi,' Leitman's voice said.

'Is the offer still open?'

'Dinner? Of course it is.'

'If it's not too late to accept, then I'd love to.'

Rawley . . . Rawley . . . Jackanory . . .

How fast can your little legs run?

He'd run all right. He'd come out from under the caravan, out from under the bumps and the bangs and he'd run.

There's no two ways about that.

Oh, yus.

But the crashes and heavings had not been what he thought they were. That's if Rawley had thought at all.

She'd been desperate, as desperate as ever in her short life, and it wasn't the red rabbit – except that it may have started it long ago.

It was within herself.

She had known it was coming. It started with the itching, then that feeling as though two great hands were squeezing her chest.

Then the first signs of breathlessness.

As usual you weren't sure whether or not it was your imagination.

But it didn't really matter which it was. It was coming anyway.

Then the wheezing. Like a blocked pair of bellows.

From the moment she had felt the itching and the tightness she had looked for the inhaler.

Paintings were everywhere. The caravan had been turned upside down and she pulled and heaved and scrabbled and threw open drawers.

It wasn't there!

And all the time the terrible itching in her chest. She scratched and scratched but she would have had to scratch through to her heart and her lungs to stop it.

The breathing became worse because of the energy she was expending. Her chest grew tighter and tighter until she was fighting for every breath.

Once before she had lost her Ventalin inhaler and they had taken her to hospital to the nebuliser machine and put a mask over her face and wired her up to a cylinder of pure oxygen.

But she was in the middle of the Forest of Dean and she was frightened for herself as she had never been frightened before.

'Rawley . . . ' she cried. 'Rawley . . . '

And Rawley heard.

He was in the bushes near the fireplace that Chris had built.

'Rawley . . . '

It was faint and hoarse. The despair and panic and fear communicated themselves easily to Rawley for they were part of his own life.

167

He crept back slowly like some frightened forest animal. The door was open. He saw her sitting up trying to suck in gulps of the good forest air – and failing.

Rawley . . . Rawley . . . Jackanory,
What is she up to now?'

Something familiar. In the mists of his own life a brother wheezing and itching.

'Oh God, it's the bluddy asthma!'

She'd made the gesture with her hand near her mouth and he had said, 'Where is it?'

'I don't know.' The words had come out as though squeezed down swollen passageways.

Then he'd found the inhaler behind a plate on the floor. She'd used it. Slowly she began to relax. She felt floaty. She lay back. She was breathing regularly. She said, 'Stay with me, Rawley.'

'I'll stay, missus.'

He sat on the other bunk, not lying down because it was her husband's. He curled himself up in his two coats with his plastic bags on his lap and his head against the woodwork.

He watched over her.

'Hello . . . This is Xxxstasy . . . your call is costing 44p a minute and 33p a minute off-peak . . . My name is Cindy. What would you like to talk about?'

'I want to talk to Barbara.'

'I'm afraid that our rules do not allow clients to nominate—'

'Don't give me that crap,' Ronnie said. 'I want to talk to Barbara, otherwise I'm going to talk to your super.'

There was the sound of muffled voices in argument and then a different voice, a frightened voice, said, 'This is Barbara.'

'This is Black Knight. I don't like that.'

'What?'

'What just happened. I don't like people saying I can't speak to you.'

'She's new. She made a mistake.'

'I know where you are, you know. I've stood outside the building and looked at the lights. I could easily visit you.'

He was lying. He had no idea where the building, which had once housed MR MAGIC – GAMES, was situated.

'I'm sorry,' she said again. 'It was a mistake.'

'Darth Vader destroys.'

'Yes, I know.'

'Guess where I am?'

'In a call box?'

'No. I'm on my bed. I've got it in my hand. I'll read what it says. On one side there is a serial number. Then in a different place it says "Made In Belgium". Funny that. With a name like Browning you'd think it would be made in England.' He held the empty gun near the phone and pulled the trigger several times.

'Did you hear that, Barbara?'

'Yes.'

'I'm going to use it, you know. On the copper I told you about. And his girlfriend too. You're going to read about it in the papers. I'm going to be famous, only no one will know – except you and me. I've been following them both for days. They don't know. He's not a very good cop. I got so close today I could touch them. In a wine bar. Arguing. You ever heard of a place called—' He suddenly stopped. 'No I mustn't say the name. That's where they're going. Somewhere in Wales, I think. But they're going to Wiltshire first. He wants to check on someone called Chris.' He rubbed his fingers over one of the bullets that lay on his candlewick bedspread. 'You still there, Barbara?'

'You're lying, aren't you?'

He felt a stab of anger.

'This is what turns you on,' she said. 'Stories like this. You haven't got a gun. You'll never kill anyone.'

He sat up on the bed and looked at the gun in his hand.

He felt a sense of outrage. He wished he did know where she was. He would go round right now and show her the gun and maybe frighten her with it.

Instead he said, 'You little bitch. You wait till you read about it in the papers.'

She must have had second thoughts for she said, 'I'm sorry, I didn't mean—'

His mother's voice said, 'Ronnie! Ronnie, where are you?'

He shouldn't have phoned from the house. There was always the chance of an interruption.

'I'll talk to you later,' he said and put the receiver down.

'What?' he called.

'I can't shout through a wall!'

'Why not? Your voice is loud enough.'

He put the gun under his pillow and went through to his mother's room.

'Well?'

'That's not a nice way to speak to me.'

The television was on. She was watching some dreary game show.

'Look, Ronald.' She pointed to the sherry bottle on the bedside table. It was empty.

'There was half a bottle there a little while ago!'

'Never.'

'There was, I'm telling you.'

'Couldn't have been.'

'You're becoming an alcoholic.'

'That's just nonsense. And don't you use that word!'

'You lie in bed and soak it up like blotting paper.'

'So would you,' she said, her voice cracking slightly. 'So would you if you were lying here. You're an ungrateful little—'

'Sod?'

'I broke my back for you. I went from door to door. Summer and winter. My God. I must have walked a million miles—'

'For one of my smiles? M-a-a-a-a-m-e-e-e . . . '

'Don't be so silly! And carrying my cosmetics sample case. And ringing a million doorbells. All for what? Look at you now. Hair down to your shoulders. An earring like a ponce. If you weren't my son, do you think I'd stay here with you?'

'With me! I like that. That's something, that is. It's the other bloody way round.'

'There you go again, bloody this and bloody that.'

He turned as though to leave the bedroom and she said, 'Ronald.'

'What?'

'You know what time of day this is, don't you, darling?' She was smiling at him.

'Yes, I know. It's sundowner time.'

'And your mother hasn't got a sundowner.'

'OK,' he said. 'I'll get you a bottle.'

'You're a good boy.'

Chapter 23

'It wasn't a case of me having an affair or Jill having an affair,' David Leitman said. 'Neither of us had anyone else. It was a marriage that had run its course.'

They were in an Italian restaurant in Wandsworth. They'd both had steaks pizzaola, shared a bottle of Montepulciano, and were now drinking their coffee.

'We talked endlessly. We were going to turn over new leaves, we were going to do this and that, we were going to see a marriage guidance counsellor, a psychiatrist. In the end we didn't.

'You see, there was nothing under the leaves we were going to turn over. We'd just grown tired of each other. I remember I used to lie in bed and think: I can't go on with this. I'm not going to be lying in this bed in this room with this woman this time next year. And I think Jill was feeling the same.

'And that's the story of my life.' He lit a panatella. 'My God, I've been talking without a break. You should have stopped me.'

'Why?' Linda said. 'Other peoples' lives are the most fascinating things on earth.'

She had heard him talk of his past: his growing up in what was then Rhodesia where his father had been a lecturer, then university in England, journalism, a spell of living in southern Spain – 'Before it became the world's greatest tourist trap' – writing short stories and a novel that wasn't published. Back to journalism., Marriage. Then finally the break with newspapers.

'That's what bothered her,' he said. 'The insecurity. The

172

fact that there wasn't a guaranteed cheque coming in each month. I'd waited until the kids were old enough to look after themselves, but she still couldn't accept it. I think she just couldn't believe that the young reporter she'd married all those years ago could make it on his own as a writer.'

'But you did,' Linda said.

'Only after we'd split up. That was what made the difference. I wasn't living with someone who didn't believe in me.'

He paid the bill and they drove back slowly through the dark streets. He opened the front door of the house and said, 'It seems odd going out to dinner with someone and then coming back to the same house.'

She smiled and said, 'Would you like to come in for a nightcap?'

'It's my turn. I've a bottle of Calvados. What about a glass?'

His apartment was . . . just that, she thought. It had everything apartments should have but . . .

'I know what you're thinking,' he said, as he looked about with her eyes.

The sitting room was monochromatic; a light brown carpet, with darker brown furniture. The room was full of autumn tints but the season was spring.

'You're thinking it needs a woman's touch,' he said.

'Well . . . some flowers wouldn't be a bad thing. And a pot plant or two.'

'I'd actually thought along those lines myself. I mean the pot plants. I thought how attractive yours were.'

'They make a difference.'

He gave her a Calvados and she said what a lovely evening she'd had.

'Me, too,' he said.

He seemed nervous. He walked to the windows, stood for a moment, then crossed to the fireplace and leaned against the wall. He was all sharp angles.

He said, 'I haven't been to that restaurant in years.'

173

'Did you take Jill there?'

'No.'

'Why did you never marry again? Men seem to.'

'I thought about it. I wanted to. But . . . anyone interesting was—'

'Married!' They said it in unison.

'True,' she said.

She heard a noise in the street below and crossed quickly to the windows. She pulled the edge of the curtains aside and looked out. The street was empty.

'What's wrong?' he said.

'I thought I heard someone on the front steps.'

He looked at his watch. 'At half past eleven?'

'George—' She stopped herself. The earlier phone call was too much of a giveaway. 'You can never tell with George. He works odd hours.'

'I didn't know he was a regular visitor.'

'He's not. I hadn't see him for a long time . . . years . . . then Susan wanted to do this trip and I couldn't manage it. I had to go to George for money. Since then he's been keeping contact.'

'Do you mind?'

'Not the odd phone call. That's how it's always been because of Susan. She's been the link. But I don't want him on the front doorstep.'

'I mentioned him to Norman Paston on the *Chronicle*. He told me that George has a big reputation as a thief taker.'

'You can get away with anything in the police as long as you're a good thief taker. But they don't necessarily make good husbands.'

He held the bottle up. 'Just a drop,' she said, passing him the small liqueur glass.

'You were going to tell me something the other day, I think, about George, but you weren't sure if we knew each other well enough.'

'I'm probably being silly. Making too much of it. But it'll give you an indication of what George is like. It's just

174

that . . . when we were first married he always thought of me as little Linda Brown. And he still does. And . . . well . . . what he meant was that . . . I wasn't the kind of woman who was supposed to enjoy sex the way a man was . . . You see, it's embarrassing talking about it . . .'

'Don't be silly. It's almost exactly what Jill once said to me. I wasn't to worry if she didn't enjoy it. I was just to ignore her. It implied a kind of duty.'

'That's what George thought. He seemed to think I was someone who was supposed to lack . . . I suppose you could call it . . . passion. But you see I didn't. And that shocked him a bit.'

David uncurled himself from the wall, sat in one of the easy chairs and stretched his long legs into the middle of the floor.

'Look,' he said, 'I think you have the same hang-up as I have. We're being nervous and strained with each other. You're worried about the two of us getting close, aren't you?'

'Yes.'

'So am I. Or I was. Not now. The point is I think we like each other and there's a certain logical progression, isn't there? Or not?'

'I suppose there is.'

'The problem is, no matter what we do now, circumstances have changed. If we do nothing our relationship will harden into an artificial one. We'll listen behind our doors to see if it's all clear before coming out. So we won't have to meet.'

'But the same applies if, well . . .'

'If things broke down afterwards?'

'That's what worries me. I've seen it happen to friends of mine. They become close to people in their own block of flats and then when it's over they can't break up naturally. And it took me a long time to find this place. It suits me. I don't want to throw it away.' Even as she was saying it she knew it was wrong.

He smiled crookedly at her and said, 'This is all a bit

cold-blooded, isn't it? We never spoke like this when we were young.'

'When we were young we didn't have so much to lose.'

'It isn't really bricks and mortar at all, is it? It's not really your nice flat. If I thought it was I'd have misjudged you badly. They're only symbols, aren't they? You're using them as an excuse.'

She paused. 'You're right. It isn't bricks and mortar.'

'It's emotions. Feelings. Being strung-out if something goes wrong.'

'I'm not sure I could cope with it again.'

'There is another way. Two adults giving each other pleasure. No strings. No one else getting hurt.'

She rose. 'I won't lie to you. I won't say I've never gone in for one-night stands. But I'm not a one-night-stand person.'

David pushed himself on to his feet. 'Nor am I really.'

At his front door she took his shoulders in her hands, rose on her tiptoes and kissed him on his cheek. 'Thank you for a lovely evening.'

He put his hand under her chin and turned her face so that he could kiss her on the mouth. She resisted for a second then she kissed him properly. She could feel a sudden jolt in his body as though she'd struck him. It communicated itself instantly to her. Rationale . . . good intentions . . . all exploded in a hunger so great she felt her legs begin to tremble. She pulled his head down keeping his mouth on hers. As they broke away they turned, arms still around each other and moved towards his bedroom. Then she heard the sound of her phone coming up the stairwell of the house.

'Don't answer it,' he said.

'I can't just let it ring.'

'Of course you can!'

'It might be Susan. She's in Australia now. It's morning there.'

They came apart and she ran down the stairs. She flung open her door and picked up the receiver.

'Linda,' a thick voice said.

176

'What do you want, George?'

'I just wanted . . . ' He was very drunk. 'I just wanted to say goo . . . goodnight . . . '

'You bastard! Leave me alone!'

She slammed down the receiver. She knew that David would be standing by his open door on the floor above. All she had to do was to walk up the stairs. But the moment had passed. She felt angry and upset. The fear that something might have happened to Susan had been real.

She went to her door and called, 'It wasn't Susan. It was a wrong number. Goodnight, David. And thanks again.'

The lights were on in the building which had once housed MR MAGIC. It was midnight and Barbara's shift had just finished. She collected her coat and went downstairs into the bleak industrial street. In the small car park the lights of a car flicked on and off. She crossed, opened the door and slid into the front seat next to Brian.

He kissed her and at the same time slipped his hand into her blouse and covered her breast.

'Not here!' she said, pulling away.

'Why not?'

'The others will see us.'

He was thin-faced, in his early thirties, with thick dark hair that smelled of machine oil. He was a printer and worked the early night-shift. He came to see her straight from work and she had never smelled anything other than machine oil. To her it was his natural smell.

He kissed her again and said, 'I been thinking of this all day.'

'This? Or me?'

'You, of course. Goes without saying.'

'No it doesn't. I like you to say it.'

He drove to an isolated area behind a building at the far end of the industrial park. Here the lights were dim and the chain-link fence was festooned with paper and cardboard.

He unzipped his trousers and placed her hand inside.

'Don't you even want to talk for a while?' she said, irritated. 'I haven't seen you for a few days.'

'What's there to talk about?'

'Why can't you be civilised? Why can't we go into the West End? Why can't we have a drink or a meal? Things don't shut down in London just because it's midnight.'

'You know why.'

'Because you've got to get home to Tracy!'

'She's expecting me. She'll have made food.'

Barbara withdrew her hand and leant back. She liked Brian. Well, *quite* liked him. She was afraid of losing him. He was all she had. He was important to her, especially when she was with her friends. She could talk about him. My boyfriend, Brian. And when they said when are we going to meet this famous Brian she would be able to say, 'He's a married man,' and it gave her a kind of dangerous glamour that the other women, with ordinary boyfriends, did not have.

But there wasn't much glamour about Brian now as he fumbled with her bra.

She said, 'You said you and Tracy were finished.'

'We are. It's not gonna be like this all the time. Don't be so—'

'So what?'

'Sitting there like a puddin'.'

'I like a little affection, a little talk. All you want to do is get it over and go back to your wife.'

'I can't help it if I met you after I was married.'

'But you could be a little more . . . romantic.'

'Don't you feel like it?'

'I would if you—'

'I thought it turned you on.'

'What?'

'These blokes that ring you.'

'Turn me on?'

'You once said it was like watching a porno film.'

'I don't like watching porno films. Anyway, this is just filth.'

178

'What do they say?' There was a sudden interest in his voice. He was always trying to get her to tell him.

'They say . . . well . . . what they want to do to you.'

'What?'

'I don't want to talk about it. It's sick. They want to use bottles . . . things like that . . . '

'Like what?'

'Is that what you want to do? Use a bottle?'

'Don't be silly!'

'Well, then don't go on about it. I hear enough on my shift without talking about it now.'

'OK.'

He tried to pull down her pants.

She felt his fingers tugging at the material. 'You'll tear them!'

'Take them off then.'

'Let's get in the back. It's too uncomfortable here.'

They got in the back and immediately he was all over her. 'Put your leg up there,' he said urgently, grabbing the ankle of one leg and putting it on the back of the front seat.

'Your hurting me!' she said.

It was all over in a matter of seconds. She put her legs down and straightened her clothing and thought, 'God, this is what they talk about. This is what everyone wants.'

He zipped up his trousers and lit a cigarette.

She knew what the next thing would be. He'd tell her how tired he was. He'd begin to yawn. Then he'd be off and she wouldn't see him again for a night or two.

She really felt like saying, 'I don't want to see you again,' but then when she looked at herself in the mirror and saw the pitting of her skin she realised she couldn't. At least someone wanted her.

'Brian.'

'Yeah?'

'One of my clients—'

'Clients! I like that.'

179

She ignored him. 'He sounds OK one minute and crazy the next.'

'Oh, yeah.'

Brian had lost interest.

'Calls himself funny names. Darth Vader. Black Knight. And he says he's got a gun.'

'Oh, yeah.'

'Brian, he says he's going to kill a policeman.'

Brian laughed and flicked the cigarette out of the window. 'And you believe him?'

'I don't know. I was wondering. Should I go to the police and tell them?'

'Tell them what?'

'What I've just told you.'

'What's there to tell. People say anything. Anyway its probably illegal.'

''Course it's illegal!'

'I don't mean shooting coppers. I mean what you're doing. This sex chatline thing. The papers made a fuss about it. They said they were going to have the law changed or something.'

'We're not a sex chatline. We're supposed to be there for lonely people. Like the Samaritans.'

'Oh yeah? I bet sex is all they talk about though.'

She thought of her supervisor, Lex. 'I suppose it is, really. Even so. You think I should? Maybe I could phone them. Anonymously.'

'What are you going to say? That someone phoned you and told you he was going to kill a copper? You don't know his name, where he's phoning from. How're they going to do anything? Anyway, if you want to get mixed up in something like this that's your business. Don't ask me.'

'I don't want to get mixed up in anything.'

'Listen, he's a loony. They're all loonies. Darth Vader! Christ!'

He yawned.

'You better go,' she said.

'Yeah. I better.'

Chapter 24

Ronnie woke early. He had set the alarm but did not need it. He felt a contraction of his stomach muscles as memory reminded him what day this was. This was *the* day. *Der Tag*, as old Daddy Crowhurst had called it when anyone was being released from the nick.

He was full of nervous energy, part anticipatory, part apprehensive. If there was ever a time it was now. London was too difficult and anyway he couldn't go on following them. They'd rumble him sooner or later. It had to be now. The sooner the better as far as he was concerned. It would complete the circle that had begun in the garden shed in north London.

Why the hell did she have to scream?

They'd charged him with attempted rape but he hadn't wanted to rape her. He'd only wanted her to watch. Like the woman on Wimbledon Common. *She* hadn't screamed even though he'd held a knife to her. She'd watched and he'd seen the fear in her eyes. That was what he really wanted according to the doctors at Granton. They'd made him admit it. Power. OK, so they were right. Didn't change anything.

All she had had to do was watch and be afraid and give him the power.

The Black Knight in full armour.

Instead the bitch had screamed and the copper had come.

He could still feel the blows on his face even now. He could feel the bone go. He could hear the kind of cracking noise nuts make in a nutcracker.

He'd nearly lost his eye.

He put his finger up to the concave scar. When he was little his mother had always called him her beautiful boy. But in ten seconds that had been destroyed. Veronica bloody Lake. Always hiding behind long hair.

Well, the time had come to repay the debt.

Der Tag.

He got out of bed and reached on to the top of his wardrobe for the box. He unwrapped the gun from its yellow duster. Unpacked the bullets and spread them on the bed.

Browning automatic.

A handgun.

He loved that phrase. Not a big gun. Not one of those bloody great things the coppers used. But big enough. It was what came out of the spout that mattered.

He put the gun up to his nose and smelled the oil. Lovely. He'd never fired a gun before. He wondered how it would feel. He held it out straight ahead of him, clamping his left hand on his right wrist.

Rock steady.

Squeeze.

He put down the gun and tiptoed into his mother's room. She was lying on her back with her mouth open, breathing hoarsely. Carefully he lifted her clock from the bedside table and advanced the time by two hours. He opened the curtains a little. It was barely light outside. The TV set had been on all night, the screen was a shower of static snow.

He shook her by the shoulder.

'Wha—?' she came slowly to consciousness, swimming upwards through the sherry layers. 'What?'

'It's waking-up time,' he said.

'Never.'

'It is.'

She turned and pulled the sheet up to her neck.

'What's the matter with you?'

It came out whassamattawisyou because her teeth weren't in.

'I told you. Look at the time.'

He was pretending this was not abnormal. In fact he never woke her. He always wanted her to sleep as long as possible.

'And I was having such a lovely dream.'

He had also had lovely dreams. Of golden sand, bucket and spade, mum and dad, the blue sea.

Then the reality. Old Crowhurst muttering in his sleep, and the grey light of day against the bars of the window.

'You gotta wake up.'

'You mad? Let me sleep!'

'You know what day it is?'

'What?'

'I gotta see my parole officer. If I don't then it's back to the nick and you're on your own.'

That woke her.

'Today?'

'Yeah.'

'But you went yesterday.'

'They was too busy.'

She pulled herself up on the pillows. Sleep was gone now.

'And what about the day before? You're always going out. Always leaving me. How can I manage?'

'Don't worry. I'll be back. You want some breakfast?'

'Why are you asking? What's all this anyway? Oh, I know. You want the car. Well, you're not having it!'

'I'm asking you nicely. You want some breakfast or not?'

'Breakfast! You couldn't make breakfast. You can't do *anything* right!' She put in her teeth and said suspiciously, 'You never asked before.'

'Well, I'm asking you now. You better hurry though 'cause I'm off.'

'Not in the car!'

'You want to go to the bathroom?'

He helped her up and took her along the passage. In the bedroom he began to search for the car keys. Every time he used the car she made him return the keys to her. 'Where the hell could she have put them? He looked under her pillows, under the mattress, among the sheets.

He began to panic.

'Ronald!'

He went to fetch her. In his hand he carried a partly full sherry bottle. Sometimes she would knock that off at lunchtime. The sun went down early in this part of London.

'What you doing with that?' she said angrily.

'I'll show you.'

He began to pour the sherry into the washbasin.

'Ronnie! Ronnie! No!'

'I want the keys.'

'Oh God, stop!'

The golden liquid with its rich grapey smell was gurgling down the plughole.

'And there won't be any more,' Ronnie said. 'I'm not going out to get any more. OK? I'd rather go back to the nick than live like this.'

'All right! Just stop!'

He stopped. She pulled the keys from her dressing-gown pocket. He took them from her and helped her back to bed.

'You wouldn't?'

'What?'

'Leave me?'

Suddenly he felt the power. Black Knight. Darth Vader.

'Shut your fucking face,' he said to her.

He went to his own room to collect the gun.

'Ronnie! Ronald! Darling!'

He stopped in the passage. 'The bottle's in the bathroom. You want it, you get it.'

Then he was out of the house in the grey dawn and into the car and away.

He drove across London to Pimlico. The streets were dead. He parked. Leo Silver's white Golf was in a resident's bay on the opposite side of the road. He leaned back in his seat and waited. He wanted to tell someone what he was doing. But who? Barbara? He'd like to phone her. He'd felt the power in his conversations with her. Real power. He'd like to talk to her and tell her that this thing that had haunted him for so long was about to be resolved.

But he couldn't leave the car in case the bloody copper came down and drove away. If he'd had a car phone it would have been different.

One day, when he was rich, he'd have a car phone and he'd be able to phone anyone and everyone. He would have the whole world at the end of a telephone.

'Are you all right, missus?'

'Yes.'

It was early morning. Rawley had woken to see her looking at him.

'That's my husband's bunk,' she said. 'You shouldn't have slept there.'

'I didn't put my head on the pillow. Not on the pillow. I wouldn't do that.'

'You must go out now. I'm going to get dressed.'

Rawley, in his two coats and with his plastic bags in his hands, a single complete world, nodded his agreement, rose from the bunk and went out into the forest.

'You can get a fire going and boil some water and I'll bring out the coffee. Have you got a mug?'

He put his hand in one of the plastic bags and brought out an old tin enamel mug, chipped and stained. He held it up so she could see it.

'All right.' She wasn't giving him one of hers again.

He broke sticks and used some of the wood he had chopped and got a good fire going. He poured water from a jerrycan into a smoke-blackened kettle and hung it over the fire. Soon it was boiling. Rachel came out in her long flowered dress with a cardigan around her shoulders and made the coffee.

'How many sugars?' She knew from the day before but made him say it anyway.'

'Four! I've a sweet tooth, missus.'

They stood on either side of the fire in the grey morning. It was chilly after the rain.

She felt strange. Light. Airy. She could sense a painting spell coming on and her thoughts raced from one corner of her mind to the other as she probed for a subject. She no longer wanted to paint the red rabbit. That was finished for ever.

'I'm an artist,' she said. 'A painter. Can you paint?'

'Rooms.'

'Is that what you were? A painter and decorator?'

He shrugged.

'I like you, Rawley. You make a good fire. But you can't stay in the caravan. Not like last night. Do you understand that?'

'Oh, yus.'

'Were you frightened last night?'

'Not when I knew. Oh, no.'

'How did you know?'

'I had a brother. He had the asthma. Died of it.'

'What am I going to do, Rawley?'

'Missus?'

'I mean, I can't stay here for ever. I'll become part of the forest. Like you. Where do you live, Rawley?'

'Live?'

'You must have had a house sometime. A wife. Children.'

He smiled inwardly.

'A mother and father? A home? You had a brother.'

'And a mother.'

'You must have had a father!' She was irritated.

'He was a sailorman. He went to sea and never came back.'

'What did your mother say then?'

'Good riddance.'

'You're like a troll. You live in the wildwood.'

'What's a troll, missus?'

'Look in a mirror. There are gingerbread houses in the

forest and woodcutters who send their children away. Is that what happened to you? Were you sent away to become a troll?'

She sat on the steps of the caravan nursing the hot mug of coffee in both hands.

'Rawley . . . Rawley . . . Jackanory . . . Would you like me to tell you another story?'

His slatey eyes shone and he sat on the damp ground near her.

'It's a story about a princess. You like them, don't you?'

'Oh, yus.'

Once upon a time there was a beautiful princess and she married a handsome prince and they were happy.

. . . happy . . .

And they pretended to be ordinary people and travelled in a land where no one knew them. They journeyed slowly along the little roads of this kingdom. They slept under the stars and washed in crystal streams and lay in soft scented grass.

Eventually they came to a great wildwood. It was then that the prince changed.

Do you know what the humpbacked beast is Rawley?

No, missus.

It's a game two people play. A man and a woman when they're alone.

And the prince wanted to play this game with the princess but she did not want to play. She wanted to be his friend. He was so kind.

I loves people who are kind.

That's when the princess became sick again and the prince said what could he do?

And the princess said that a spell had been cast upon her by the evil Dragon of the North and she asked the prince to kill the Dragon – only then would she feel free to play the humpbacked beast with him.

Rachel began to cry. Rawley was embarrassed.

187

She wiped her eyes on her sleeve, picked up the small hand-axe and began to split a log into kindling.

Rawley waited. The story could not be over. It was like an unresolved phrase in music. He felt jangled and tense.

'What happened, missus?'

'He shouted at her. He called her mad. Then he took the horse and left her alone in the wildwood. Don't you think that's a sad story?'

'A sad story. Oh yus, a sad story.'

She threw out the coffee dregs and rinsed the mug. 'It's time for prayers,' she said. 'Come along.'

Macrae was feeling frightful. The general debilitating and nauseous effect of the whisky he had drunk the night before combined with the gloomy certainty that he had made a bloody fool of himself with Linda.

He dressed as he made himself coffee. He'd run out of sugar and it tasted foul but at least it was hot.

His thoughts kept on returning to the conversation he had had with Linda. She had changed. That's what he couldn't understand. Going out with a bloody writer! It wasn't like her. She wasn't the sort of person writers took out.

He thought of her in bed with Leitman and to the gloom, headache, sore eyes and belief that death was just around the corner, was added a sullen rage. Part of that rage was focused on himself for ever having let her go, being stupid enough not to see her potential.

The phone rang.

'Macrae you bastard!'

It was his second wife's voice.

'For God's sake, Mandy, whatever it is not *now*!'

'Your effing cheque bounced!'

'What?'

'Don't give me that! You knew when you signed it!'

'Listen I thought—'

'Yeah, I'll bet. You thought a little roll in the sack would make up for it. Well it doesn't. I told you before, the kids

188

are growing up. They need things. And listen, Macrae, in case you don't know it, there's a new law going through that gives me the right to have child support taken off your salary before you even see it. Think about *that* while you're signing the next cheque!'

'Mandy!'

But she slammed down the phone at her end and Macrae was left looking at the black mouthpiece of his.

And so it was with a mixture of feelings, all of them dark, that he reached Cannon Row. It was then that he remembered that Silver wasn't there, that he'd gone swanning off in the middle of a case – forgetting, for the moment, that it was he who had pressed him to go.

All he could think of now was that he was lumbered with additional work and a strange assistant. Macrae did not take lightly to organisational change, and especially not this morning when what he really felt like doing was creeping back to his house and getting into bed.

' 'Morning, sir.'

' 'Morning, Mr Macrae.'

' 'Morning, guv'nor.'

He nodded briefly at the faces who were greeting him.

The desk sergeant said, 'There's a message for Leo Silver.'

'He won't be in today. Is it about the Healey business?'

'It's about some villain called Purvis. Wanted me to check on his whereabouts.' He gave Macrae the message sheet.

Detective Chief Superintendent Wilson came into the room and said, 'George, have you seen the Deputy Commander yet?'

'No.'

He took Macrae aside and said softly, 'Get it over with. It'll only make things worse postponing it.'

'I'm not in any mood to see Scales.'

He brushed past Wilson and went down the corridor to the incident room which had been set up to investigate the abrupt and permanent departure of Robson Healey.

More than twenty detectives were at their desks working on the case.

He said to the sergeant in charge, 'Where's this young genius Geddes who's supposed to work with me?'

'I haven't seen him this morning, guv'nor.'

'Christ. Listen I'm going to get some coffee then I think we must do something about friend Harris. I want him brought in. Put the frighteners on a bit. Did Silver say anything about this?' He gave him the message sheet. 'Has it got anything to do with Healey?'

'He didn't say anything to me. Purvis . . . Doesn't ring a bell.'

Wilson, who had followed Macrae into the incident room, said, 'Purvis and Silver. It rings *some* sort of bell. What's his first name?'

'Ronald . . . '

'Mr Macrae!' The voice rang down the aisles between the desks. Macrae turned and saw the Deputy Commander standing in the doorway. Scales's face was pink. 'I'd like to see you in my office.'

He turned. Macrae looked at Wilson, who dropped his eyes. Various detectives held their phones to their cheeks and looked at him too. They knew.

Macrae flushed, then followed Scales down the corridor to his office. It wasn't like last time. There was no George this and George that. Not even an invitation to sit down. Scales sat behind his desk leaving Macrae standing.

Scales let the silence grow. Then he began to fiddle with his ball-point pen. Click . . . Click . . .

Macrae thought: The little prick's been reading psychology manuals.

Slowly he took out his packet of cigars and lit one.

Scales looked on appalled, then, leaning back, pointed with his thumb at the no-smoking sign on the wall behind his chair.

'Do you mind!' he said.

Macrae feigned total surprise. 'No, I don't mind.'

190

Chapter 25

'Heigh-Ho, Silver!' Zoe said from the passenger seat of the Golf as they went skimming down the M4 towards the West Country. 'This has got to be better than working.' She put her hand on Leo's thigh and began to stroke it.

'Don't touch me there unless you kiss me first,' he said.

'You know, I don't mind now about splitting the holiday. In fact I rather go for it. Two holidays are better than one.'

'Are you watching for the turn-off?'

'Naturally. The Chippenham exit. Should be coming up in a couple of miles.' She paused and said, 'Leo?'

'I hear you.'

'You're not going to be fishing *all* the time, are you?'

'Why not? What else is there to do?'

'You sod.'

They turned off the M4 and travelled north for twenty minutes. 'There's the sign,' she said. 'Lympton. Eight miles.'

'Never been here before.'

She looked at the deserted countryside and said, 'Nor has anyone else.'

'Eddie Twyford would hate it. He hates the country.'

The sun was pale behind a layer of cloud and there was a light film of rain on the windscreen.

'Can you fish in rain?' Zoe said.

'All the best fishermen do.'

'Oh.'

They reached Lympton and Silver slowed down. It was a picturesque village and would not have appeared in guide books. It straggled crookedly between dull fields cereals. There was no redeeming feature: no spire, no

He looked round saw an ashtray filled with paperclips, emptied them on to the desk and ground out the panatella. It made a nasty, smelly mess.

Scales got out of his chair, picked up the ashtray, took it over to the window. He opened it and tipped the contents out.

An angry voice rose on the morning air. 'Watch what you're doing, you silly fucker!'

Scales pretended not to hear and regained his seat. 'Communications are everything in police work,' he said. 'Would you agree?'

Macrae was host to two warring voices; one told him to take Scales by the scruff of his neck and throw him into the Thames. The other, the voice of survival, said, 'Cool it!'

He cooled it.

'Aye, sir.' This time he did not accentuate the word 'sir' but gave it a texture of subservience.

Scales looked up, startled.

He gathered himself and said, 'And communication between senior officers is vital. I thought I'd made myself clear last time about Twyford. I said he was no longer to be your driver. Do you agree with that?'

'With what, sir?' Macrae's voice was mild.

'That that's what I said.'

'Yes, sir, I agree.'

'OK, then.'

Click . . . click . . . went the pen . . .

'But the communications seem to have broken down.'

'It won't happen again, sir.'

'What? Oh. Yes . . . well . . .'

Click . . . click . . .

Scales changed tack in the face of Macrae's attitude.

'You see, George, I can't let you have a driver if no one else has one. You do see that, don't you?'

'Yes, sir, I see it.'

'OK . . . then . . . It isn't right. I mean Twyford's got his own work to do.'

Click . . . click . . .

'And the money. I mean costs are just shooting up. Take the copier. That's another thing. Everybody uses the photocopier for private business. They all copy their football coupons. I was sent here to save money. I'm not having it!'

'No, sir.'

'Sit down, George.'

Macrae sat.

'Anyway, what I wanted to say to you—'

At that moment Les Wilson burst into the room. 'Excuse me, Kenneth,' he said. 'But something's come up!'

Scales rose instantly. 'What, Les?'

'It's about Sergeant Silver.' He turned to Macrae. 'Ronald Arthur Purvis. I thought it was familiar. What's Silver's girlfriend's name?'

'Zoe.'

'What's all this?' Scales said.

They ignored him.

'Zoe!' Wilson said. 'That's right. And Purvis was—'

'Yes!' Macrae said. 'He was the little shit who was put away for attempting to rape her. He's the one that Silver beat . . . That's how Silver met Zoe!'

'Right!'

'Will someone please explain?' Scales said, coming round his desk between the two men.

Macrae said, 'This bastard, Purvis, had her in a shed. Silver heard her screaming.'

'Jesus!' Wilson said. 'He's been released.'

'What's the problem?' Scales said.

Wilson filled him in. Scales grew suddenly grave. This was the sharp end.

Macrae was remembering Silver telling him about the envelope with BOLTOP printed on it that had been addressed to Zoe.

Would he?

Some of them did.

Best make sure.

Macrae said, 'Excuse me.'

He went to the front desk, gave the sergeant the message sheet and said, 'Get hold of this bird's parole officer. Find out where he's living.'

Scales and Wilson followed. Scales said, 'I think you should get hold of his parole officer. Find out where he lives and—'

Macrae ignored him and went into his own office and closed the door. He picked up his phone and dialled an internal number. 'Eddie?'

'Yes, guv'nor.'

'Come round as quick as you can.'

manor house, just a collection of buildings in which people either worked or lived or farmed. Puddles of brown water dotted the roadside. Notices said 'Mud on the Road', there was a great deal of cowdung and a ripe agricultural smell.

'Mmmmm,' Zoe said, taking a deep breath. 'Love that country air!'

Leo ignored her. 'That's just what I was hoping for,' he said, pointing at a narrow brick house with a little blue sign outside it which said, simply, 'Police'.

'The thin blue line,' Zoe said.

'A country copper. The most dependable bloke in the world. You remember those old Ealing movies? These blokes were always riding around on bicycles keeping the peace and doffing their helmets. Nothing like them. Old England to the letter. I won't be long.'

Silver walked up the short front path. There was no garden, the small lawn was rank. The bell did not work. He knocked on the half-open door but there was no reply.

'Anyone at home?'

He pushed the door and went in. The small living room was to his right. He put his head in. Two easy chairs covered, in what looked like mock tiger skin, faced a large, shiny television set. On a table beneath the window was the remains of breakfast.

The sound of voices was coming from the rear of the house and he walked through into a kitchen warmed by a small range. The kitchen window overlooked a larger piece of un-kempt grass at the back where a man and a woman seemed to be doing a kind of dance. Then Silver saw that they were holding something between them. It was an oval mirror in a gilt frame.

Each was struggling to take it away from the other and the woman was shouting: 'You bastard! You bastard! It's mine! It's mine!'

Over and over.

This scene was being watched by a second woman who stood some distance away looking on passively.

Silver had only been watching for a few seconds when the struggling woman tripped, fell, and brought the mirror on to the ground with a crash. The frame broke. Bits of glass fell into the long grass. She rose on to her knees, stared at it, then before the man could react, she picked up a large rock and ran across the yard.

'Beth!' the man shouted. 'Don't you bloody dare!'

She ran towards a white Ford parked in the drive. He tried to block her way. She swung the rock at him. He leaped backwards.

'I'm telling you, Beth, I'll—'

In two strides she was at the car and had brought the stone down on the windscreen. It crazed and a hole appeared over the steering-wheel.

'Beth! You bloody bitch!'

The other woman had not moved an inch.

Beth dropped the stone and ran up the back stairs of the house. She saw Silver in the kitchen.

'Who the hell are you?'

She was in her late thirties or early forties, he thought, with a square face that might once have been handsome, framed by unsuitable ringlets of hair. Her eyes were red from weeping.

Silver opened his mouth to tell her and she said, 'Are you with Evie?'

'No. No I'm not.'

'God damn her!'

She turned and walked out of the front door. Silver went after her. 'I'm from London. The Metropolitan Police. I wanted to see—'

'My husband. Sergeant Christie. God rot him!'

She went out of the gate, turned into the road and was lost to sight.

Silver went back into the house. 'What do you want?' the man said.

Silver identified himself and began to wish Macrae had been with him. Christie was big, bald, and had a kind of sandy quality. The other woman was with him. She was much younger than his wife and pretty in a kind of blousy, bucolic way. Her dark hair was cut in a bang and her breasts were her main feature. They reminded Silver of the second Mrs Macrae.

'You all right, darl?' Christie said to the woman.

She looked past him and smiled at Silver. The smile said, 'See? I've won.'

Christie said, 'Christ Almighty! You can never tell with women. And that's the truth.'

He went to a cupboard and took out a bottle of ginger wine and two glasses. 'Need something after that.'

Silver tried to stop him but it was too late. 'Here's to crime,' Christie said. 'What can I do for you?' He glanced over at Evie. 'Is this confidential?' he said to Silver.

'No. Not really. 'It's about Chris Nihill. I want to talk to him.'

'Chris who?'

'Nihill.'

'Here?'

'Is there another Lympton in Wiltshire? Upper Lympton or Lower Lympton?'

He shook his head. 'Only this one.'

'Well, that's the name we were—' A voice inside his skull said, 'No, it wasn't. Nobody had said his name was Nihill.'

He tried to recall, as clearly as he could, what Rachel had said. 'I know he's a carpenter,' he said. 'Part gypsy.'

'Mitchell. There's a Chris Mitchell. He's a carpenter. The last time I saw him was just before he left for a job near London. That was, oh, months ago. Joinery business, I think.'

'And horses. He knows about horses.'

'I'm told he was here the other day with a horse.' He turned to Evie. 'That's right, isn't it, darl?'

She smiled again at Leo and this was taken by Christie to mean assent.

'That's what they do best. Trade horses.'

'Tell me about him.'

'Well . . . you know these people. Typical. He's a wanderer. But unlike most of them he's not very bright.'

'How do I find them?'

Christie rolled himself a cigarette, lit it and then said, 'Go straight on through the village. Take the left fork. There's a big stand of trees. Beeches. Ash. You'll find them there. The whole bloody tribe of them.'

Silver thanked him and rose.

Christie said, 'Don't often get London coppers down here. Never had one – not to my knowledge.' Then, as if a sudden thought had struck him, 'What did you want to see him about?'

'Just want him to corroborate a statement.'

'If there's anything I should know about I want to know. This is my patch.'

'Of course.'

'I mean I don't want . . . ' His mood had changed to one of veiled belligerence. 'I don't want people coming here and telling me how to do my job.'

'Never dream of it.'

Silver said his goodbyes. Christie frowned at him. Evie smiled. He wondered if she ever spoke.

At the car he held up a hand to Zoe. 'Don't ask. I'll tell you later.'

He drove through the village and took the left fork. As Christie had said there was a stand of trees. Among the trees was a group of mobile homes on concrete plinths. In a field nearby there were half a dozen horses.

Silver turned off the road on to a track and drove into the trees. A man in the field schooling a horse was the only human being he could see. Then, as though conjured up by magic, figures began to appear through the trees. They were mostly men, but some women, arms folded, stood a little distance away and watched.

There were half a dozen men, dressed similarly in what looked like the trousers and waistcoats of old suits. Most wore hats. One man carried a shotgun. They came up to the car and surrounded it.

'Woops,' Zoe said.

Silver got out and identified himself. The hostility instantly increased. He felt he had suddenly entered a foreign country. It had begun with Christie. But at least he was recognisable. These men, with their swarthy faces, did not seem to be part of the English countryside on a spring day.

One of the men, big and barrel-chested, asked him what he wanted.

'To see Chris Mitchell if he's here,' he said.

'For what?'

Suddenly Silver thought: how would Macrae deal with a situation like this?

The one thing he wouldn't do was let them scare him.

'Are you the boss?' Silver said.

'What d'you mean, the boss?'

'You understand English, don't you?' There was the faintest ripple of reaction. 'I mean, you're the one who's doing the talking, that's why I asked. I want to talk to Chris Mitchell if he's here.'

'You better take him to Maggie,' one of the men said.

The barrel-chested man stared at Silver and Silver stared back at him. Then he said, 'Come with me.'

Zoe leapt quickly from the car. 'I'm coming too.'

The three of them walked across a patch of grass littered with pieces of old cars and stopped before the largest of the mobile homes. A few pots near the door were filled with plastic flowers. In the window was a large bird cage in which there was a pair of budgerigars.

'You wait here,' the man said.

A few minutes later he came out and motioned them to enter.

A woman in her late sixties or early seventies, with hennaed hair piled high on her head, dangling earrings and a face that once might have been beautiful, sat in an easy chair smoking a long cigar and reading the paper.

'What you want to know about my grandson, Chris?' she said.

Silver absorbed his surroundings. The place was filled with knick-knacks. Outside, the group of men had formed up under one of the windows.

'What you want with Chris?' she repeated. 'If you come about that horse, he got it honest. For work done.'

'I didn't come about the horse,' Silver said and began to understand the basis of the hostility.

'What then?'

'I wanted to talk to him about the woman he was with. Rachel Nihill.'

'What about her?'

'We're making some inquiries, that's all.'

'What's Chris got to do with them?'

She fixed him with a pair of black beady eyes and Silver wondered if she carried a knife. In books and movies gypsy women always carried knives.

'I can assure you, Mrs . . . Mitchell, is it? I can assure you that we don't think Chris has done anything wrong. All I want to do is ask him a few questions.'

She seemed to relax.

'Did he mention her to you?'

She nodded. 'Said she was mad as a March hare.'

'Why was that?'

'Wouldn't give him his conjugals. Oh, I know they wasn't married. But if you lives together the man has expectations. I know. I lived with four. I've eight sons and three daughters. And twenty-seven . . . no, I lie. Twenty-eight grandchildren.' She waved an arm at the group outside. 'Most of those are mine. You can't tell me about conjugals.'

'He told you this?' Silver was surprised.

'Not him. He wouldn't like to shock me. No, his brother did. But he told me about the asthma. And how wild she got. Painting and painting.'

'The red rabbit.'

'That's it. Rabbits. Chris couldn't put up with that for long.

He's a good boy but he's a man, if you knows what I mean. A man expects his conjugals.'

Silver thought he heard Zoe snort behind him.

The woman pulled on her cigar. 'He done her caravan up and they lives together in every other way. He told his brother she used to get undressed in front of him. Well, I mean that's more than flesh and blood can stand. They lived together but not together, if you know what I mean. So finally they has a row and he takes the horse. His payment see. He was here for a few days then he went back to the caravan to get his tools.'

'And now?'

'He said he was going back to the joinery near London. That's where you'll find him.'

She tapped on the window and the barrel-chested man put his head in the doorway. 'They're all right, Billy,' she said. 'You can take them to their car now.'

They drove slowly out of the encampment, slowly back through the village, slowly past the policeman's house, and then Silver put his foot on the accelerator and they shot down towards the M4.

After about five miles he pulled in at a lay-by. Zoe flung her arms around him. 'Leopold Silver! You were magnificent!'

A small white Mazda passed them but they didn't notice it. It pulled on to a farm track about a mile ahead of them and stopped out of sight behind a hedge.

After a moment Silver untangled himself and said, 'I was, wasn't I?'

'Wow. I thought they were going to lynch us.'

'So did I.'

'You're my hero.'

'There's something all wrong with this thing.'

'No conjugals, that's what was wrong.'

'That and a lot of other things. I've been unhappy about Rachel since we saw her. But I couldn't put my finger on it. Then there was the second interview with her mother. Listen. Let me recap.'

201

'You sound like a game-show host. Drive and recap. I'm getting hungry – and thirsty.'

'OK.' He drove back on to the M4 and headed for the Severn Bridge.

'Here's a young woman who hated her parents. 'Specially her father. Couldn't wait to get to boarding school. Didn't want to go home in the holidays. She starts off by being a beautiful child, ends up as a plain teenager with asthma. The moment she gets a chance, i.e. grows up and inherits some trust-fund money, she leaves home permanently. Goes to art school near London, meets a carpenter – probably the first male she's ever dominated – falls in love, or something similar. Calls herself Rachel Nihill and lets us believe that the carpenter is called Nihill when his real name is Mitchell. Why?'

'Unless she wanted people to think they were married.'

'Why not call herself Mrs Mitchell then?'

'You have me there. Unless it's part of her wish to dominate him. She makes up a name and makes him adopt it.'

'Maybe. The police sergeant said he wasn't very bright.'

'Go on.'

'OK, they travel through the West Country with her getting undressed in front of him but the DO NOT TOUCH notices are all over her.'

'No conjugals.'

'Exactly.'

'They fetch up in the Forest of Dean. They have a row about something.'

'Maybe he didn't like her paintings.'

'He takes the horse called Nemo and comes back to Lympton.'

'Leo—'

'Hang on. Nearly finished. So maybe he sells the horse to his grannie or one of his multitudinous relations. Goes back to the caravan to pick up his tools, says goodbye to Rachel Nihill-Healey and goes back to the joinery near London – where he worked before – leaving her with a caravan, lots of paintings and a dead kitten. That's the story anyway. His disappearance worries me. The timing is just too convenient. Unless he's on the run.'

'Leo, you never told me about the dead kitten.'

'Is it important?'

'Stop for a moment.'

They were coming on to the bridge approaches and he pulled to the side.

'Listen,' she said. 'You never told me that the horse's name was Nemo either.'

'So?'

'So what do you know about asthmatics?'

'Nothing, thank God.'

'Well, I'll tell you one thing, no asthmatic in his or her right mind would have a kitten or a dog or any other animal like that which might be likely to cause an allergic reaction and bring on an attack. That's one thing that's odd. But what about these names? Didn't you take Latin?'

'No. Did you?'

'They said it would come in handy one day. Listen, *nemo* means no one. Take the "l" away from Nihill and you've got *nihil*. Which in Latin means nothing. And the caravan was called Erewhon which is nowhere. Right?'

'Right.'

'How about this: If you were trying to erase yourself, change not only your name but your whole being, how about a surname meaning nothing, a moving house called nowhere, pulled by no name, the horse. For goodness sake, Leo, she was trying to disappear. Even from herself.'

'And Erewhon meant Utopia. That's what she was looking for.'

'And then it all went sour.'

'I think I want to talk to her. The Forest of Dean's only twenty or thirty miles out of our way.'

'I'm hungry.'

'OK, we'll eat in a place called Lexton. The caravan's nearby.'

Chapter 26

Macrae and Eddie Twyford were met by a uniformed sergeant in a patrol car.

'Is this the house?' Macrae said. It was one of a terrace of small villas in north-east London and even though Eddie had put all his expertise into the drive, it had taken them the best part of forty minutes to get there. So Macrae had radioed for help and the patrol car was waiting.

'Yes, sir.'

'Seen anyone?'

'No, sir. Everything quiet.'

'You been round the back?'

'I was told to watch the house. That's all, sir.'

There was no garden in the front. It had been tarmacked and oil spillage told that it was a hardstanding for a car.

Macrae, followed by the sergeant and Eddie, went up the front path. The house had been built at the turn of the century and had the typical small panels of coloured glass on either side of the door. It was only two floors and Macrae thought he knew the layout for it was not dissimilar to his own house.

He rang the doorbell. He rang it again. He rattled the letter-flap. He went to the bow window and, shielding the reflection on the glass with his hands, he peered in. The room was a standard front parlour. The furniture was dark and the room was gloomy.

'Let's go round the back,' Macrae said.

The two men followed him along the path at the side of the house. The rear was a junk yard of old tins and plastic. A washing line sagged on its poles.

Macrae looked through the back windows but all he saw was a kitchen with unwashed dishes.

He returned to the front and stood on the sill of the downstairs bow window then climbed gingerly on to the sergeant's shoulder but he could not reach high enough to look through the first-floor window. He came down and stared at the front door.

'Can you open it?' he said to the uniformed sergeant. 'Have you a sledgehammer?'

'A sledgehammer?' The sergeant looked shocked.

'All right, laddie, force it.'

The sergeant examined the door and was about to put his shoulder to it when Macrae said, 'This isn't television. You'll end up in hospital. Break the glass.'

He broke one of the glass side panels, reached in and unlatched the door. They went in.

'Jesus!' Eddie said, putting a handkerchief to his nose.

'Not very nice, is it?' Macrae said.

The passageway smelled strongly of drains and rotting food.

Macrae mounted the stairs. There were two bedrooms and a bathroom on the floor above.

He stuck his head into the first bedroom but it was empty. Then he went into the second. An elderly woman was lying on the floor in a tangle of sheets and bedclothes. A dozen or more pills of varying colours were scattered on the bed and the carpet. Macrae bent over her. He could not detect any sign of life. He told the sergeant to radio for an ambulance.

He went into the bathroom. A partly empty bottle of sherry was standing on the washbasin.

He went into the second bedroom. The bed was unmade and on the floor next to it was a cardboard box and a yellow duster. On the bed itself, caught up in a fold in the sheet, was a single bullet. He picked up the duster and, above the smell of the room, he could detect a different smell: gun oil.

He looked through the cardboard box and found assorted papers, some were pages torn from notebooks. Underneath them were three photographs. One was of Silver and Zoe walking along a street, the two others were street shots of Zoe alone. There were several newspaper clippings about the trial of Ronald Arthur Purvis and one of a London murder case in which Macrae and Silver had been involved.

Macrae and Eddie had discussed the possible scenario in the car. It was Macrae's contention that no matter how twisted the mind, how long the brooding, how deep the need for revenge, the fact was that most criminals did not seek out the policemen, judges, or jurymen who sent them to gaol and try exact an eye for an eye.

But you could never tell.

Not when the man had been beaten so badly.

Now Eddie said, 'What d'you think, guv'nor?'

'He could be any bloody where,' Macrae said. 'Look at this!' He picked another torn page from the box. 'He must have been making notes. He's written down . . . I can't make it out. It looks like . . . Paxham. That's where . . . Oh, Christ!'

He grabbed the phone and got through to Directory Inquiries. 'The Paxham Arms,' he said. 'It's in Paxham. On the Welsh borders somewhere.'

The unhurried voice gave him the number and he dialled.

'Give me the manager.'

'I'm the owner,' a voice said. 'Will I do?'

Macrae identified himself. 'Has a Mr Silver checked in yet?'

There was a pause. 'No. Mr and Mrs Silver haven't arrived yet. Is anything wrong?'

'Listen carefully. When they do I want you to tell Mr Silver . . . '

He paused, thinking of Zoe.

'Yes?'

'Tell him that the desk sergeant has a message for him.'

'The desk sergeant?'

'That's right. For God's sake write this down.'

'Yes. Of course.' He repeated what Macrae had said.

'And the message is in reply to his request . . . ' He sought for the words and phrases that might give Silver a clue about what was happening, without frightening Zoe.

'In reply to his request . . . ' repeated the voice.

'Listen . . . tell him that that Detective Superintendent Macrae is bringing the message to him. Got that? Because he needs to see him. Tell him not to go fishing or leave the pub.'

' . . . not to leave the pub.'

'Read it back to me.'

The voice read it back. 'OK,' Macrae said. 'How long does it take to get to you from London?'

'Depends how fast you drive.'

'Fast.'

'Three hours.'

'I'll be there in three hours.'

He told the uniformed sergeant to get on to Les Wilson and tell him to alert the Somerset and Avon police and then have someone guard the house after the body had been removed.

Then he said to Eddie, 'Come on, let's go.'

The Black Horse was the only pub in Lexton. A sign said, 'Bar food. Home cooking.'

'Home cooking! I bet it's from Swindon and microwaved,' Zoe said, as they parked. 'Anyway, who the hell wants home-cooking when you go out? French home-cooking perhaps, but not British.'

'Fuss, fuss,' Leo said.

It was a gloomy day and the interior of the pub, a series of small interconnecting alcoves each with black settles and a table, and lit by small shaded lights, was dark enough to make them pause while they became used to it. But it did have a fire and Zoe immediately went towards it, rubbing her hands.

She was dressed in her new 'country' wardrobe. It reminded Silver – though he was wise enough not to say so – of the kind of gear an explorer might have worn for a final assault on one of the Poles: a blue beanie on her head, a red quilted anorak, ski trousers and Ugg boots.

'I might want to walk home if I get fed up with you,' she had said, darkly.

They were the only two in the place and the publican and his wife were behind the bar cleaning glasses. They were both large and Dickensian. His face was framed by grey muttonchop whiskers and he wore a red bandana round his neck. His wife wore a fisherman's smock. It was clear they saw themselves as 'characters'.

'Not too good,' the publican said, tilting his head at the great outdoors.

'Except for ducks,' his wife said, in a Welsh accent.

This was something Silver had noticed before: country folk never said hello, they always opened a conversation with a remark about the day.

'We came through some rain,' he said, accepting the tradition.

'Where from?'

'London.'

'Ah.' He made it sound as though it was in some remote land. 'You'll find Lexton a bit quiet after London.' Then he winked.

Leo ordered a couple of glasses of wine. The woman behind the bar said, 'If you're thinking of having lunch, my love, it's all on the blackboard. Except there's no plaice and chips. Couldn't get any fish this morning.'

Zoe and Silver studied the blackboard. There were all the familiar old enemies: lasagne, chili con carne, stuffed baked potatoes . . . '

'Is it really home-cooking?' Zoe said, innocently.

The publican set up the glasses of wine and said, 'Everything cooked by my wife's fair hands.' He winked again.

'Well . . . ' the woman said.

'I feel like bangers and mash,' Silver said.

'I can do you that. I've got some nice spicy pork sausages.'

'Make it two,' Zoe said.

They stood at the fire drinking the wine but were near enough to the bar to be able to talk to the publican.

Silver said, 'I was here a few days ago. There was a young woman in a caravan in the woods. Gypsy caravan. Do you know if she's still there?'

'I haven't heard she's gone,' said the publican.

'Never comes in here,' said his wife. 'Her friend did though.'

'The hippy,' her husband said.

'For goodness sake. Any young man with long hair is a hippy to Fred. He's a carpenter.'

'Bunny will believe anything,' Fred said. 'If he's a carpenter I'm a . . . I dunno what . . . Anyway you best ask Rawley. He'll know.'

'Rawley?' Silver said.

'Rawley's been hanging about with her,' Fred said with a wink at Leo and Zoe. 'Haven't you, Rawley?'

He looked past Silver, who turned and followed his glance. In a dim alcove behind them there was a faint rustle and Leo could make out a figure he had missed before. At first all he could see was a bundle of clothing, then a face and eyes. He looked like a tramp.

'What say you, Rawley, old sport?' said Fred. 'Your girlfriend still down in the forest?'

Rawley moved again, feeling for his two plastic bags under the table. He did not speak.

'You going to marry her, then, Rawley?'

'Leave off, Fred. Don't tease him.'

Fred winked again.

'I'm not teasing him. I just want to know if Rawley's going to make an honest woman of her. What's she like, Rawley, old sport? I was told she was some sort of painter. You been helping her paint?'

'That's enough, Fred!' She turned to Leo and Zoe. 'He likes to tease people.' She turned to Rawley, 'You all right, my love? You want something? Half of mild?'

She pulled half of mild into a straight-sided glass, carried it over to Rawley's table and returned to the fire. Standing with her back to him, she said, softly, 'I don't like to see him teased.'

'Who is he?' Zoe said.

'Rawley? He's a local. Born here. In the forest. When the mining was still going. My family came here when I was a little girl so I've known Rawley all my life. He's not as simple as people think and there's no harm in him. We knew his family for many years. There were two boys. One died. Rawley was brought up by his mother. She took in washing. Poor Rawley. He never quite got to grips with life. Did odd jobs and things like that. Then he, well, they say he began to hear voices.'

'And he was carted off to the loony bin,' Fred said, with a wink.

'Not so loud!' Bunny said. She turned back to Leo and Zoe. 'Then a couple of years ago he was released.' She turned to Rawley and said, 'It's all right, my love, you can drink it. It's on the house.' She resumed her description. 'He knows the forest inside out. Often sleeps out there.'

There was a movement at Rawley's table. He was trying to pick up his glass but his hands were shaking so much that he finally gave up and left it where it was and bent his head to sip from it.

Rawley . . . Rawley . . . Jackanory . . . What did your little eyes see?

He managed, after several tries, to get the glass up into his hands and took a long pull. He wiped his mouth on his sleeve.

'That's the trick,' Fred said.

'Want another one, my love?'

She fetched his glass and Fred drew him another half pint. She put it on his table.

'Prayers,' Rawley said.

'What's that, my love?'

210

'We must pray.'

It was said so softly Leo almost missed it.

'Who must pray?' Leo said.

Rawley said, 'Oh God . . . Oh God . . . ' Then, 'I runs. I runs . . . and runs . . . '

'You been running, my love? You shouldn't do that at your age.'

'I'll give you three wishes,' Rawley said, his voice slightly stronger.

'Who?' said Fred. 'Give who wishes?'

'The princess.'

'Of course,' Fred said, winking at the group near the fire. 'There's always a princess. Tell us the three wishes, Rawley.'

'Leave him alone, Fred.'

'Come on. What were they?'

' "What is the first wish, said the prince—?" '

'Oh, so there was a prince too was there?'

'Fred!'

'There's always a prince. Come on, old sport, what did the prince say?'

'He said . . . he said . . . '

Rawley stopped and drank . . . then suddenly he put his hands to his ears as though to blot out all noise . . .

'I told you,' Bunny said. 'He hears voices.'

There was a call from the kitchen and the sausages and mashed potatoes were put on a table near the fire. Silver and Zoe ate with relish. Rawley sat with his hands to his ears for a few minutes, rocking back and forth, then he seemed to gather himself. He picked up his drink and took another large swallow.

Suddenly, he said, 'Once upon a time there was a prince . . . '

'You telling us a story now, Rawley? It's like that programme on the television for the kiddies.'

'Rawley likes children's TV, don't you, my love?'

But Rawley was not listening. 'Once upon a time there was a prince and he wanted to play the humpbacked beast . . . '

211

'The what?' Fred said, and winked.

'Rawley,' Bunny said. 'Don't you start being filthy now. Otherwise out you go.'

'She loves him . . . She says she still loves him . . . Even though . . . ' His voice tailed away. Then he turned and looked at Leo and said, 'I hears voices. In my head. Oh, yus.' He was crying.

Embarrassed, Leo paid up quickly and they went out to the car. He drove slowly through the village, past the store where he had earlier asked the way, found the track and began to go down it. It was muddier than before. He remembered how difficult Eddie had found it and decided not to chance it.

'You stay here,' he said, pulling up on the grass.

'You must be crazy,' Zoe said looking around at the gloomy trees.

'I'm not going to be long.'

'Leo—!'

'It's thick mud and you'll wreck your boots.'

'Leo—!'

'Anyway, you'd probably inhibit me. So just do what I ask.' His voice was harder.

'You bastard!'

He got out of the car and began to walk into the forest in the direction of the caravan.

Chapter 27

Ronnie was sitting in the little Mazda about fifty yards from the Black Horse. He had a clear view of the pub door. He had seen Silver and Zoe go in, now he saw them come out. He felt under his seat and reassured himself that the gun was still there. His hand was slimy with sweat and he could feel a dampness on his body and face.

The fact was – and Ronnie had grown increasingly aware of it – the fact was that he was afraid . . . scared shitless. It had come on him gradually. When he had first watched the two of them come out of the house in Pimlico he had felt euphoric. It was all meshing. It was all coming right. The plan was perfect.

He had followed them to the M4 and along the motorway, he had followed them to Lympton and watched and waited and driven ahead of them just like the police did on television.

Even that had been all right because he had had to keep so far away from them he had not been able to see Silver clearly.

But then he had followed them down the last section of the M4 and had been just behind them when they stopped suddenly at the Severn Bridge and he had had to pull up quickly. That was when he had seen Silver in close-up and the fear had begun to seep into him.

Of course he'd been close to Silver before. He'd followed both of them in London. Had stood only yards away from them in the Old Vienna. But that was different. It was part of the game. Now the game had ended and what old

Crowhurst had called the nitty gritty had arrived and Ronnie didn't like it.

Silver looked so . . . what the hell was the word . . . 'competent' . . . ? Don't kid yourself. It wasn't 'competent'. The word was 'dangerous'!

He watched as they crossed the pub car park. Silver walked easily, lightly. He was dressed in black. Darth Vader. The Black Knight. Oh Christ!

Ronnie fingered the indentation on his cheek. He'd only tangled with Silver once and this is what had happened to him!

It was one thing lying on your bunk in the nick and planning what you'd do when you came out. Everybody knew that that was what sustained you in there. Kept you going. Kept you sane.

And at home it'd been the same. He had his 'collection' there. That had made a difference. His 'exhibitions'. Laying the weapons out on his bed. The death star, the knife, the Browning automatic made in Belgium. I mean, Jesus, just holding the gun made him seem . . . invincible.

He'd thought of Silver as the 'target'. Somehow that made it seem less dangerous. You shot at targets, they didn't shoot back. But this target was flesh and blood and was dressed in black and suddenly it wasn't just some inanimate object.

He wished he was back at home right now having an exhibition and looking forward to telephoning Barbara. That had been great. Telling her about the gun and everything.

He was abruptly angry with himself.

Come on . . . come on . . . for Christ's sake, you'll never get another chance like this.

But what if he's also got a gun?

But the British police don't carry guns. Anyway, he's on bloody holiday.

Come on . . . come on . . .

He saw the white Golf turn down a side lane.

Come on!

He started the car but his hands were so sweaty he could

214

hardly grip the wheel. It's no good, he told himself. Even if you had them covered you'd probably not be able to hold the gun properly.

Look, its no bloody go. You're too worked up. Too tense.

Of *course* there'd be other times. Maybe he could get her alone some time in London. Wait for her. Follow her from the Underground or from a bus.

Yeah.

That was it. This was too dangerous. Who the hell was going to look after his mother anyway if something happened to him?

It was just bloody irresponsible. He was all she had. He couldn't go risking himself like this.

No, better put it off. Wait for a better moment. Plan it better. Practise with the gun. He could afford to shoot off a few bullets . . .

You don't have to do anything!

You can leave at any time and they won't even know.

That gave him a lift. He'd followed them all the way from London and they didn't even bloody know! The stupid sods!

Then he had a brilliant idea. A reign of terror. Envelopes and letters. Phone calls in the night. God, he'd make their lives a misery.

Terrific.

He'd work it all out on the drive back to London.

He started the engine and drove past the entrance of the lane that led down into the forest.

And then he saw a sight that made him change all his plans. Zoe was getting out of the car. Silver was nowhere to be seen. She seemed unsure of herself, unsure whether or not to go down the track.

Ronnie had no idea what they were doing, only that at this moment she was alone. He turned down the lane and cut the engine.

* * *

215

'Leo!' Zoe called. 'Wait for me!'

Even as she was locking the car she thought: this is silly. I'm in the country now. But if you lived in London you locked your car and old habits died hard. By the time she had finished he had vanished.

She knew the direction. It was only a matter of staying with the path. But the path was muddy. It sloped gently downwards and had become a channel for rainwater.

'Leo!'

Ugg boots, which were soft sheepskin with the fleece on the inside were more like sloppy slippers, and were not quite as explorer-ish as Leo had thought them. They slipped and slid, absorbed water, became covered in mud, and she was forced to leave the path and look for drier, grassier areas.

She scrambled down the slope, trying to remain parallel to the path, but in the nature of forests her own line was constantly interrupted by branches or boulders which caused her to make little detours. Soon she could no longer see the path, was no longer quite sure where it was or what her own position was.

'Leo!' she called.

The day was dark and the forest smelled of damp leaf-mould. She didn't like it at all. She decided she had been foolish and that she should go back to the car.

Then she heard a noise behind her and thought: *Leo, you bastard, you're playing games!* She turned. It wasn't Leo.

'Zoe!' the man said, softly.

That took a moment to sink in.

It was so unexpected that she had not registered her own name for a few seconds.

'What—?'

'Don't you recognise me?' Ronnie asked.

'Why should—?'

She half turned, looking for Leo, and he grabbed her hair in one hand and she saw the gun for the first time in the other.

'If you scream I'll kill you,' he said.

'You're hurting!'

He laughed nervously and dragged her towards a thicket.

'Don't . . . '

'You'll hurt yourself if you struggle.'

His fingers twisted in her hair and tears started in her eyes. He dragged her into the thicket.

He threw her to the ground. She fell upon a formation of woven branches and heard them crack.

'You recognise me now?' he said, pulling the hair away from his face.

'Yes . . . '

The terror was there and yet it was not there. This was a dream. Lightning never struck twice in the same place.

'I've been waiting for this,' Ronnie said. 'We were rudely interrupted the first time.'

He was drenched in sweat. It dripped down from his forehead and he could taste the salt as it slid over his lips. The gun felt as though it was covered in oil, which it was. The oil and the sweat were combining to make it slippery.

'Kneel,' he said.

'Please . . . '

The black-and-white newsreels showed kneeling figures being despatched with single shots in the head then tumbling into communal graves.

Ronnie saw her terror then. It was what he had been waiting for. He saw it in her eyes and he felt the power.

He began to unzip his trousers.

She knew what was about to happen.

It was the indignity of it that enraged her. The fact that he made her kneel and face him, that he was going to make her give him . . . her mind veered away from the phrase.

Anger gripped her.

She did not see the gun as a threat; it did not have the menace of that earlier knife. It seemed unreal. Instead of kneeling, she launched herself at him clawing and flailing. His hands were occupied. The gun slipped from his fingers

217

and fell on to the grass. Then they were wrestling and twisting and, finally, falling.

She fought with all her strength, trying to use her nails on his face. He fought back, fear giving him added strength. He was suddenly terrified. This was not meant to be happening! This was not what he had planned for. He wanted to get away from her, to run.

But she was wiry and strong and moved like lightning. His face was pressed into the leaf-mould. He saw the eye. Only one eye at first. Leaves covered the other. Then the tip of a nose. Black hair. Lips turned back over earthy teeth. He screamed and jerked away. A hand like a claw seemed to grip him. Not Zoe's, but a hand stained by dirt and rain. The ground under him wobbled. He screamed again and scrambled to his feet, trying not to stand on whatever was there.

He turned to run.

The figure was black against the sky.

Darth Vader.

The Black Knight.

The light glinted on the axe.

He bent for the gun. The axe began its descent. He fired once, and then he felt the crushing blow as the blade bit into his collar-bone and ate deeply into his chest.

The Black Knight was on his knee. Ronnie fired again.

Rachel fell sideways.

Ronnie stumbled away into the forest trying to staunch the blood that poured from his terrible wound.

And Zoe was left with Rachel's dying body and the face and the nose and the hair that floated in the leaf-mould and the dead eyes that stared up at the rainy sky.

Chapter 28

'But why?' Mrs Healey said, tears streaming down her face. 'Why would he kill my Rachel?'

It was evening in the Welsh border town of Chepstow. A glimmer of late sun on the Severn Estuary and a cold wind blowing.

But in police headquarters it was almost too warm. Someone had switched on the heating earlier in the day and the air was stale and dry.

Four people were in interview room number two: Silver, Zoe, Macrae – who had caught up with them late in the afternoon after terrorising the owner of the Paxham Arms and finally locating Silver on the car radio through the local police – and Mrs Healey, who had driven down from London to identify her daughter's body.

She was a different person from the one who had identified her husband. Now she was broken, a woman who looked twice her age instead of someone who had never looked as old as she was.

As Macrae examined her he saw eyes red and puffy from weeping and a face that had grown haggard. He did not think that Harris would be keeping her company much longer.

His glance touched Zoe, then Silver. Zoe was flushed, but calm. He recalled how panic-stricken she had been the last time and how Silver had had to create a safe world and place her in its centre before she began to throw off the horrors.

This time the horror had been worse, yet she had come through it better than Silver.

Macrae was worried about him. His skin was the colour

of putty. His eyes were bright, almost glittering. His hands were shaking slightly and he had asked Macrae for a cigar, something he had never done before.

The long day was coming to an end. They'd got what they could out of Rawley and they had interviewed the woman in the Lexton shop who had sold Rachel the heavy wrench. The only loose end was Purvis. A large force from the local police was at present combing the Forest of Dean for him and road blocks had been set up. They knew he had been badly hurt and Macrae had been told that the dogs had been called in and were probably going into the forest even as they talked.

Mrs Healey's question remained hanging in the air. *Why did he kill my Rachel?*

It was the word 'my' that stuck in Macrae's throat. Death changed a lot of things, he thought, but it couldn't change the facts. All it did was produce guilt, oceans of it.

Earlier he had interviewed Mrs Healey by himself. He hadn't been rough, there had been no need, because she'd been rough on herself – perhaps for the first time ever.

He had taken her back to when Rachel was a child and heard about the abuse. For a man with three children, two of them daughters, it came hard to Macrae. He had to control his anger and disgust.

Only once did he allow his feelings to burst out. 'God!' he said, 'What sort of man was he? How can a man destroy someone as close to him as his own child?'

She had said bitterly, 'Close? Robson was never close to anyone. He was a stranger to Rachel.'

They went through it all step by step because it was in Rachel's childhood that the later tragedies, like the small beginnings of tropical storms, were formed.

'Was the asthma psychosomatic then?' he said.

'Probably. But it's never as clear-cut as that.'

'But you knew! Couldn't you have stopped it?'

'He simply denied it. Said she was lying. Said I was mad.'

Macrae did not reply and she took this as an accusation – which it was.

'You never knew him!' she cried.

She told him of several instances when her husband had used violence against business rivals, burning down their offices, sinking their ships. She told him how he had come down to the cottage and beaten up Collins. He had got his heavies to hold him while he smashed his teeth with a piece of firewood.

And that was the progression: fear leading to terror, leading to inertia, leading to guilt. And as far as Rachel was concerned: fear leading to illness, leading to madness, leading to murder.

The actual killing of Robson Healey would never be definitively set down, Macrae knew, because both players were now dead. But as far as the evidence could take them it seemed that Rachel had bought the wrench from the shop in Lexton, caught a train to London and gone to her father's house. He'd been expecting Lucy Spilsbury. Had gone up to his bedroom, perhaps to finish dressing. Rachel had accompanied him and killed him.

But why? That was what Mrs Healey had wanted to know. Why had she left it all this time?

Silver said, 'I think her boyfriend, Chris Mitchell, tried to rape her. That's what we've got out of Rawley and he says she told him. She took him to the grave and she prayed and told him what had happened as a kind of fable. And that's when he saw Mitchell's body in the shallow grave and he ran away. And not too long after that we met him in the pub.

'Rachel and Mitchell had been living together as man and wife, as intimately as any two people could live – except for a sexual relationship. She wouldn't allow it. And he wouldn't put up with that indefinitely. So he tried to, or succeeded, in raping her. And she killed him.'

Suddenly Zoe said, 'Chris . . . Christopher . . . Aren't people called Christopher sometimes nicknamed Kit?'

'Kitten!' Macrae said.

Mrs Healey looked up, mystified, but Silver went on, 'And she must have thought that she would never, never be normal while her father existed because of what he had made her do. So she had to kill him, too!'

Macrae looked doubtful. He hated psychology. He'd have been much happier if one of his underworld narks had come along and said, Mr Macrae this is how and why it happened . . . And told him.

But Silver was developing his theme: 'She suffered from a psychosomatic illness as well, don't forget. I mean, both things could be laid at her father's door. If he was eliminated, she might achieve normality, both physically and mentally. *He* was the block. *He* had to be removed. At least that's what Rachel's subconscious might have told her.'

'Maybe, laddie,' Macrae said. 'We'll never know for certain.'

They talked on. Darkness came. Statements were taken and signed. Tea and coffee were brought. Macrae found some whisky.

Finally, at nearly midnight, it was over.

Mrs Healey left for London. Macrae and Eddie went back to the Forest of Dean to see if Purvis had been taken. Silver had wanted to come too but Macrae had said, 'Go fishing. That's an order.'

'Come on, darling,' Zoe said, taking his arm as they walked through the deserted streets of the town to pick up their car.

'I think we'd better go back to London,' Leo said.

'Why?'

He didn't reply but she knew the reason.

'Look. I'm all right. Nothing happened to me.'

But he was remembering . . . He was hearing the shots again . . . and running . . . and suddenly coming upon them in the thicket of elder bushes. He'd seen Purvis with blood pouring down his chest . . . He'd seen Rachel's body . . . He'd seen Zoe, dirt-stained, her clothes and hair awry . . . And he'd seen the horror amid the dead leaves . . .

All she had ever asked of him was that he protect her – and he had failed.

He felt himself begin to shake violently.

She stopped and took him in her arms.

'Leo . . . Leo . . . They'll get Purvis. It's only a matter of time. Don't you understand? I'm not frightened any more.'

'But I am,' he muttered. 'And that's the problem.'

As Eddie drove the big Ford towards Lexton, Macrae too was brooding about Silver's problem. He would have to watch him carefully, for he had seen this kind of thing before. It was called stress.

Problems! Christ, they all had problems. His own, now that the case was almost closed, came crowding back: Mandy, Artie Gorman – he knew that wasn't wrapped up as neatly as Artie thought – Scales, Linda . . .

After a while he said, 'Eddie, it's just possible I mightn't be able to keep you as a driver.'

'What, guv'nor?' The tone was alarmed.

'I'm not saying I definitely won't, but the Deputy Commander's on my back.'

'Oh.' Then he turned to Macrae and said with a kind of forced optimism, 'He won't worry after this case, guv'nor. Not for a while anyway. When a thief taker's successful no one's going to rock the boat. Anyway, think how good it'll look for him.'

'Don't bet on it, Eddie.'

There's light at the end of the tunnel.

It was a phrase his father had often used when Ronnie was small. It was his way of saying, 'There's always a silver lining.'

It used to make his mother angry.

'Micawber!' she would shout. 'That's what you are! Always waiting for something to turn up.'

Light at the end of the tunnel.

That's what he was seeing now.

He'd been unconscious for hours. Now, like a wounded animal, he began to crawl towards the light.

It was an old-fashioned red telephone box at the side of a forest road. It lit up the darkness.

He crawled into it and forced himself on to his feet.

He was dizzy.

He closed the door behind him. The effort brought a gush of blood from the wound. It ran down his clothes on to the floor.

He wanted to talk to someone. Just to talk. To say hello. He had money in his pocket. The whole world was at the end of the telephone line.

But who?

It took him nearly ten minutes to bring the coins out of his pocket. Slowly he put in enough to phone halfway round the globe.

He propped himself up against the wall of the kiosk and dialled without conscious thought.

'Xxxtasy,' a voice said. 'This call is costing 44p a minute and 33p a minute off-peak. My name is Sharon. What would you like to talk about?'

Slowly and with care he said, 'I want to talk to Barbara.'

'I'm sorry but we can't take calls for individuals.'

'I want to talk to Barbara.'

'Caller, I'm sorry but our rules . . . '

'I want . . . ' There was a long silence.

'Are you there, caller?'

'I want . . . to talk . . . to Barbara . . . '

He began to slip down on to the floor.

'I'm sorry, but Barbara doesn't work here any—'

That was all he heard. It was all he ever heard.